"Help me out here, Hannah. Kiss me, and help me show my son that it's not enough to make you stay in Destiny."

The sheer masculinity of Dev stole the breath from her lungs.

Part of her wanted to know what it would feel like to kiss the guy all the girls had wanted. If the experience was horrible, she could stop wondering about it. But if, as she suspected, the sensation was akin to a religious experience, the memory might be worthwhile. On some dark, cold, lonely night, she could pull out the recollection and wrap it warmly around herself....

* * *

DESTINY, TEXAS

by Teresa Southwick

Dear Reader,

September is here again, bringing the end of summer—but not the end of relaxing hours spent with a good book. This month Silhouette brings you six new Romance novels that will fill your leisure hours with pleasure. And don't forget to see how Silhouette Books makes you a star!

First, Myrna Mackenzie continues the popular MAITLAND MATERNITY series with *A Very Special Delivery*, when Laura Maitland is swept off her feet on the way to the delivery room! Then we're off to DESTINY, TEXAS, where, in *This Kiss*, a former plain Jane returns home to teach the class heartthrob a thing or two about chemistry. Don't miss this second installment of Teresa Southwick's exciting series. Next, in *Cinderella After Midnight*, the first of Lilian Darcy's charming trilogy THE CINDERELLA CONSPIRACY, we go to a ball with "Lady Catrina"—who hasn't bargained on a handsome millionaire seeing through her disguise....

Whitney Bloom's dreams come true in DeAnna Talcott's *Marrying for a Mom*, when she marries the man she loves—even if only to keep custody of his daughter. In *Wed by a Will*, the conclusion of THE WEDDING LEGACY, reader favorite Cara Colter brings together a new family—and reunites us with other members. Then, a prim and proper businesswoman finds she wants a lot more from the carpenter who's remodeling her house than watertight windows in Gail Martin's delightful *Her Secret Longing*.

Be sure to return next month for Stella Bagwell's conclusion to MAITLAND MATERNITY and the start of a brand-new continuity—HAVING THE BOSS'S BABY! Beloved author Judy Christenberry launches this wonderful series with *When the Lights Went Out...* Don't miss any of next month's wonderful tales.

Happy reading!

Mary-Theresa Hussey

Mary-Theresa Hussey
Senior Editor

Please address questions and book requests to:
Silhouette Reader Service
U.S.: 3010 Walden Ave., P.O. Box 1325, Buffalo, NY 14269
Canadian: P.O. Box 609, Fort Erie, Ont. L2A 5X3

This Kiss

TERESA SOUTHWICK

SILHOUETTE *Romance*®

Published by Silhouette Books

America's Publisher of Contemporary Romance

To Sandra Ferguson, Sherry Davis, Judi McCoy and Mary Karlik. I'm thankful that y'all kept my "Texas voice" under control. And my profound gratitude for taking this Southern California refugee (I'm still not sure if we decided that makes me a Yankee carpetbagger) under your wing.

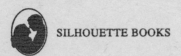 SILHOUETTE BOOKS

ISBN 0-373-19541-9

THIS KISS

Copyright © 2001 by Teresa Ann Southwick

Visit Silhouette at www.eHarlequin.com

Printed in U.S.A.

TERESA SOUTHWICK

is a native Californian who has moved to Texas. Living with her husband of twenty-five years and two handsome sons, she is surrounded by heroes. Reading has been her passion since she was a girl. She couldn't be more delighted that her dream of writing full-time has come true. Her favorite things include: holding a baby, the fragrance of jasmine, walks on the beach, the patter of rain on the roof and, above all, happy endings.

Teresa has also written historical romance novels under the same name.

SILHOUETTE MAKES YOU A STAR!
Feel like a star with Silhouette.
Look for the exciting details of our new contest
inside all of these fabulous Silhouette novels:

Chapter One

She'd forgotten how good trouble looked in worn denim, scuffed boots and a black Stetson.

Hannah Morgan stood on the bottom slat of the white, split-rail fence and watched Dev Hart's tall imposing presence dominate the corral where he supervised cutting horse training. With his back to her, she was still safe from his notice. Yet she had an unobstructed view of his assets—muscles, wide shoulders and a spectacular cowboy butt.

She hadn't seen him since high school. So why would she think of him as trouble?

Maybe it had something to do with the way those soft jeans clung to his lean hips and muscular thighs. Or that intriguing indentation in his chin. She couldn't see it from where she stood, but ten years worth of remembering produced an instant visual. His brown eyes, too. She recalled they were dark and smoldering. A woman was at risk of going up in flames from just a single glance.

Not her, of course. She was a doctor now, and practically the same skinny blonde he had never acknowledged outside of their physics tutoring sessions.

He turned around and she knew the moment he spotted her. His laserlike gaze scanned the enclosure, passed her by for just an instant, then swung back, settling the full force of his male observation on her. A small smile turned up the corners of his mouth, sending a shiver from the base of her neck to the tips of her toes.

Over his shoulder he said to the other cowboy, "That's enough for today, Wade. Feed and water him, then turn him into the corral."

Hannah's heart beat a little faster as Dev ambled toward her. Was there a sexier, more masculine sight than a Texas cowboy ambling? If so, she'd never seen it. He let himself out of the fenced enclosure and came to stand in front of her. Quickly she updated her decade-old memory. He was taller, broader, filled out— and most important—not that teenage boy any longer.

Dev Hart was a man.

If the butterflies in her stomach were anything to go by, she was still the same awkward sixteen-year-old girl she'd been the last time she'd seen him. But she held her ground, or rather her rung on the fence. She might have grown up in a trailer and worn cast-off clothes from the thrift store, but she wouldn't give him any reason to look down on her. Even though his six-foot-two-inch height would allow him to stare his fill at the top of her head.

"Hannah?" His tone held surprise that was just this side of shock. "If I hadn't known you were coming, I don't think I would have recognized you."

"Hi, Dev. Have I changed that much?"

"Yeah. How long has it been?"

"I haven't been back in about six years," she said. "But I think it's been longer since we last saw each other."

She knew for a fact she hadn't seen him since high school graduation ten years before.

"The blond hair and blue eyes are the same, but everything else is a whole lot more grown up," he said, touching the brim of his hat politely. "Polly said you wouldn't be here until tonight."

Her mother managed his household. After her father had walked out on them, Polly Morgan had cleaned houses, including Dev's parents', to support herself and six-year-old Hannah. A year before, Dev had hired her as a full-time housekeeper.

All through college and medical school, Hannah had dreamed of giving her mother a better life. She blamed herself for the fact that Polly had had to work so hard and vowed to make her mother a lady of leisure. She was on the brink of doing it, too, if she got the job in Los Angeles that she wanted, with the prestigious pediatric group.

"I got an earlier flight and rented a car at the airport. Where's Mom? There wasn't anyone up at the house."

"She took Ben to story hour at the library in town." He shifted his boots in the red dirt, then folded his arms over his chest.

Her mind raced, searching for something to say to fill the silence. This was her first trip home since her mom had taken over his household. Hannah had known she would see Dev, but she hadn't expected to have to make conversation with him, alone, right off the bat. Polly was supposed to be here to run interference.

"How old is your son now?" she finally asked.

"Almost four. Next week as a matter of fact." His wonderfully shaped mouth turned up at the corners. "He's an active little son of a gun. I don't know what I'd do without your mother. She's pretty special."

"You won't get any argument about that from me," Hannah agreed.

She knew he and his wife had split up, but not the details. When she'd heard, her first thought had been that golden boys have problems just like scholastically gifted geeky girls who grew up on the wrong side of the tracks. Her second, that it would be hard on his little boy. She knew from firsthand experience what it was like when a parent turned their back on a child.

He shoved his hat up with a knuckle and she noticed that the glow of fatherly pride lingered in his eyes. She couldn't help wondering what kind of parent he was. Memories of her own father were memories she tried to forget.

"How are you?" she asked.

"Fine. And you?"

"Good. Although I'll be better when I get an offer from one of the medical groups that I interviewed with. I'm just waiting to see which one wants me."

"Who wouldn't want you—the smartest girl who ever graduated from Destiny High," he added, his eyes sparkling with surprising interest.

"I don't know about smartest, but skipping a couple grades was probably noteworthy," she agreed.

"Are you going to be here long enough for the high school rodeo championships?"

"To be honest, I'd forgotten about that. When are they?"

"Four weeks away. And if I were you, I'd watch my step after a remark like that. In this neck of the woods, forgetting rodeo is practically a hanging offense.'' There was a smile in his eyes.

She laughed. "Yeah, Destiny is nothing if not rodeo country. How is the stock business?'' she asked.

Ten years ago, it had been profitable and she assumed that hadn't changed. Dev's family made a better-than-good living supplying stock to rodeos all across the country as well as breeding and training cutting horses, and raising cattle. He was the guy all the high school girls wanted, as much for his money as his looks. If he hadn't needed her to tutor him, they probably never would have crossed paths, let alone spoken. Of course, after each session, he'd never looked at her or claimed any association at all when they passed in the school hallways.

He folded his arms over a pretty impressive chest. "Business is better than ever. Keeps me busy. Which is why I'm so grateful to Polly. If I didn't have her to watch over Ben, the home part of this homestead would have come apart faster than a fat man's britches.''

Hannah laughed. "She adores your son.''

He angled a hip toward the fence and rested his elbow on top. "She did say you're unattached and it doesn't look like you're going to have kids any time soon. She claimed she needed to flex her grandmothering muscles while she's still young enough.''

Annoyance cut through Hannah, and she wasn't sure what bothered her more. That her mother had talked to Dev about her, or that he knew she had no one special.

"How are your folks?'' she asked, changing the subject with what she hoped was scalpel-like precision. Her personal life, or lack thereof, was not something she wanted to discuss with Destiny High's infamous chick magnet.

"They're traveling from coast to coast in a motor home. It's what they always dreamed of doing and hadn't made time for. After Dad's heart attack last year, they decided not to put it off. He retired and turned the business over to me."

"Good for him." In all of her medical training rotations, she'd seen patients forced back to work by economic circumstances when they should have taken off more time for their health. She looked beyond the corral at the red Texas dirt covered by scrub and mesquite as far as the eye could see. "But of course he could afford to. Everyone says that this is the biggest spread in Destiny."

"Everyone says?" He frowned. "You've seen the place." It wasn't a question.

"Nope." She shook her head. Her mother worked for his family, but always during Hannah's school hours. And she hadn't been back for several years. Polly had visited her in L.A. "You must be thinking of one of the other girls who followed you around adoringly."

That had popped out more bitterly than she intended. Funny how coming home brought these feelings to the surface.

"Times have sure changed," he said, shaking his head. "And I mean that in a good way."

"Are you trying to tell me you didn't like all that female attention?"

"Do I have stupid written on my forehead?" he asked, grinning. "I liked it a lot. But that was a long time ago. I've got better things to do now. Running the place and being a father doesn't leave time for a whole lot else."

"Is that so?" Why should that surprise her? Still, it

wasn't fair to peg him as the same selfish teenage guy she'd known. She had grown up. He must have too. After all, he'd married, become a father and divorced. And he'd had the good sense to hire her mother.

That was the good news. The bad—her mom was a live-in housekeeper and had sold her own home. She'd said it cut down expenses. More bad news—on this visit to her mother, Hannah had to stay on the Hart ranch, under Dev's roof.

But when she'd arrived, she glimpsed the house from the outside. It was a really big roof and her mother had said there was a separate wing for the hired help. Still Hannah knew she would have to see Dev. For the life of her, she didn't know what she would find to talk with him about. They had nearly exhausted all topics of conversation in the last few minutes, and her crack about adoring girls had no doubt put her on the verge of wearing out her welcome already. She'd taken classes in medical school dealing with bedside manner, but they didn't include polite interaction with the opposite sex. Her training had taught her to be assertive, but had been sadly lacking in diplomacy. In other words—she was socially backward. Which could be why she was still unattached.

"Look, Dev, I don't want to take you away from your work. I'll walk back to the house and wait for Mom there."

"You're not keeping me. I've got time to show you around the ranch now if you'd like to see it. I can have Wade saddle up a couple of horses."

"No thanks," she said, a little too quickly. "But if you're sure it's not an imposition, I wouldn't mind the walking tour."

"You have something against riding?"

"Not in a plane, train or automobile."

"You're afraid of horses?" he guessed.

She nodded. "I fell off when I was a kid."

In addition to being a brainer geek, her subsequent apprehension around horses had always made her feel like a fish out of water in ranch country. Just one more thing to prove that she didn't quite belong anywhere. If there was anyone else who'd grown up in Destiny and was scared of horses, she would like to meet them. All two of them could form a support group.

"In spite of that, I don't freely admit to being afraid of anything." She met his amused gaze. "I prefer to think of it as a failure to overcome a high IQ. It's not especially smart to voluntarily climb up on top of an animal who could squash me like a grape."

He nodded, but there was a twinkle in his eyes. "It's because of the whole physics thing, right?"

"What does physics have to do with it?"

"A body in motion tends to stay in motion unless acted upon by an outside force."

"Yes, but—"

"Or a body accelerates at thirty-two feet per second per second."

"You remembered. And here I thought I was wasting my breath all that time." She couldn't help smiling. "Except I believe I said objects—because the principle holds true for a feather or a bowling ball."

He'd had the oddest, sort of intense look in his eyes both times he'd said "body." And she saw his gaze slip from her face to the chest of her white T-shirt which now felt transparent, then lower still to her khaki pants and white tennis shoes. When he looked her in the eyes again, his held a gleam that she didn't understand.

Oh, she hadn't just crawled out from under a rock. She'd been around the block and guys had come on to her. But this was Dev Hart. If their past history was anything to go by, he barely knew she was alive. So how could she trust a look like that coming from him?

He rested his hands on lean hips. "You're not my tutor anymore. You're a doctor now. Don't you think bodies are more interesting than bowling balls?"

His look amped up a notch. She hadn't expected it from him, or her response—a sort of quiver that started in her abdomen and spread outward generating heat as it went. He'd never looked at her that way in high school. But then, other than their tutoring sessions, he hadn't looked at her at all.

When Dev Hart was involved, she was much more comfortable discussing physics than bodies and searched for a way to go back there.

"The fact remains, I prefer to have both feet planted firmly on the ground. That way a horse can't put me in motion for the hard ground to finish me off."

"That's true," he agreed. "But it's a real shame to let one fall stop you. Nothing compares to the exhilaration of riding."

This was just dandy. After ten years she'd finally gotten his attention and they were talking—about her deficiencies. "Surely you have better things to do than baby-sit me."

"Actually turnabout is fair play. Thanks to you I managed to get through high school physics and into college. The least I can do is teach you how to ride."

"Believe it or not, I've gotten by quite nicely without knowing. There isn't a lot of opportunity to climb on a horse in Los Angeles. Not to mention that there are safer ways to get where you're going."

While they'd been bantering, another cowboy had entered the corral leading a saddled horse. From the corner of her eye, Hannah had noticed him climb up on the animal's back and registered the clip-clop of hooves as he walked him around. Suddenly, the horse reared, startling the rider who lost his grip and fell with a grunt into the dust.

When the cowboy grabbed his shoulder with a groan and didn't get up, Dev's relaxed posture disappeared as he instantly went into action. He quickly opened the corral gate and Hannah followed right behind. They ran to the man's side and knelt down beside him in the dust.

"What happened, Newy?"

"Something spooked him. Caught me off guard—" He stopped and sucked in a breath as his leathery face tensed with pain. "Mean, ornery, lazy cuss. That dang horse just trotted easy as you please right back in the barn," the man said through gritted teeth. His sweat-stained hat lay beside him and his thin brown hair stood up in tufts on his head.

"Is it the same shoulder? Dislocated?" Dev asked. The man's pale blue eyes met his boss's as he nodded then groaned.

"Are you sure it's not broken?" Hannah asked.

The cowboy shook his head. "Happened before," he grunted. "If I hit it just right—" he stopped and clamped his teeth against the agony "—it goes out on me."

"The integrity is compromised," Hannah diagnosed, knowing the original trauma rendered the joint more vulnerable.

"Dang horse hasn't got integrity," he protested, then

grimaced in pain as he held the injured shoulder while he rocked from side to side.

"Dang physics," she said, meeting Dev's worried gaze. "That pesky hard ground has a way of acting on a body that isn't pleasant." She looked at the injured cowboy. "Do you mind if I have a look at it?" she asked.

When skepticism lasered through the man's discomfort, Dev said, "Newy Tubbs, this is Hannah Morgan—*Dr.* Hannah Morgan."

"Lady doc?" The cowboy met his boss's gaze. "I don't know—"

Hannah tried to decide what his prejudice was—that she was a woman, or hardly looked older than a high school senior. It wouldn't be the first time for either.

Dev lifted his hat and ran his hand through short brown hair before replacing it. "We can load you up in the truck and bounce over every rut and pothole between here and Doc Holloway's office in Destiny. Or Hannah can—"

"Have a look-see," he clarified reluctantly. "Okay."

Must be one rough ride, she thought, surprised he'd given in so easily. Dev moved aside to give her room. Hannah gently probed the man's injured shoulder and the protrusion that told her it wasn't broken. "It's dislocated, all right. A first-year med student could make the diagnosis."

"Guess we'll have to take you in to see the doc after all," Dev said.

"Excuse me. Didn't we just establish that *I'm* a doctor?" She met Dev's gaze. "Unless, of course you'd *rather* torture this poor man with a trip into town? If not, I can take care of him right here."

Newy appraised her doubtfully. "Little bitty thing like you?"

"He's right," Dev interjected. "Doc's done this before. I'll go get the truck and—"

"Doesn't take strength, just leverage," she assured the injured man. "What have you got to lose by letting me try? Unless you're afraid of a little pain," she challenged, looking at her patient. "But then, it's gonna hurt like hell anyway on the trip into Destiny, *and* for a whole lot longer."

He glanced at his boss, then back at her and nodded reluctantly. "Go ahead."

Hannah nodded, then gripped his wrist and upper arm. "This is going to hurt a bit," she said, bracing herself. "But I guess you already know that if it's happened before."

As he nodded, she gave a quick tug on his arm. He bit back a yell and groaned. Then he looked at her, obviously surprised. "By golly, I think that's got it. The pain's lettin' up."

She sat back on her heels. "That's what happens when it's where it should be." Without looking away from her patient, she snapped an order. "Have you got something for a sling? That arm needs to be immobilized."

Newy shook his head. "No need, ma'am. There's a first-aid kit in the barn. Wade's workin' over yonder and he's wrapped me up before." Dev helped him to his feet and the cowboy looked down at her as he cradled the injured arm to his chest. "Much obliged, ma'am, I mean Doc," he said with a wan smile.

"You're welcome."

She stood beside Dev and watched the cowboy walk

to the barn. Then the rancher met her gaze. "Much obliged."

"Don't mention it." She covered her eyes to shade them from the sun and smiled up at him, glad that he'd seen her as competent and not just a yellow-bellied coward who was afraid of horses.

He folded his arms over his chest. "What can I do to thank you?"

"There's no need. It's what I'm trained to do."

Before he could respond further, the sound of running feet caught their attention. Hannah turned and saw a pint-sized cowboy hurrying as fast as his little legs could go. On his heels and trying to keep up was her mother.

"Hi, Daddy," the little guy yelled when he was still a few yards away.

"Ben," Dev called back.

He took her elbow to guide her from the corral. Hannah fought the urge to yank her arm away from the sizzle that swept over her shoulder and down into her breasts. Pulling back would show weakness. And if there's one thing being the youngest in her class through college and med school had taught her, it was to never let anyone see that you weren't completely in control.

So she let him guide her out and watched him latch the gate, the muscles in his back rippling beneath his fitted cotton shirt. She swallowed the sound of female appreciation that rose in her throat, but the corresponding flutter in her stomach gave her trouble. It was as if she was plummeting down the longest drop on a roller coaster. She struggled for a facade of sophistication and polite, but cool interest, because inside she was ga-ga and hot enough to melt diamonds.

She watched Dev watch his son run toward him. The man's lean, strong, muscular body tensed and somehow she knew he was bracing for impact. Several moments later, the little guy hurtled into the strong arms waiting for him. Dev held the boy close for a moment, then unselfconsciously kissed his cheek while he settled his son on his forearm and ruffled his brown hair.

"Hey, squirt," he said. "Did you and Polly have fun?"

The boy nodded. Then he noticed Hannah. He pointed. "Who's she?"

"It's not polite to point, Ben. This is Polly's daughter, Hannah."

Her mother joined them, a little out of breath. "Don't you remember, Ben? I told you she was coming today. She's a doctor. Hi, honey."

"Hi, Mom." Hannah went into the arms her mother held out. *Now* she was home. It was several moments before they had hugged their fill and stood side by side, arms around each other's waists. Hannah noticed Ben was still watching her.

The boy's eyes grew wide. "Do you give people shots?"

"Sometimes. But only if it will help them feel better."

He rested a small arm around his father's strong neck and gave Dev's shoulder a couple of pats. "I don't like shots."

"Me either," Hannah agreed.

"Me either," Polly said.

Pleasure swept through her again, feeling her mother beside her. She'd been a teenager when Hannah was born and was still a young, attractive woman. People often said they looked more like sisters than mother and daughter—the same blue eyes and blond hair. Hannah had always been grateful that she didn't take after her father.

For a moment, she rested her cheek against her mom's. "It's so good to see you. I've missed you."

"You're too busy to miss me," Polly answered, chuckling, "but it's sweet of you to say so. You're a sight for sore eyes. But too thin."

As if on cue, Ben announced, "I'm hungry. Is it time for an afternoon snack yet? Aren't you hungry, Daddy?"

"I am," he agreed, meeting Hannah's gaze. "How about you? You've had a long trip."

"Starved." She stared at his mouth, the fine chiseled shape. Before she could stop the thought, she wondered what it would be like to kiss Dev Hart. It was an absurd idea, but she couldn't help thinking about what those smiling lips would feel like pressed against her own. She shook her head to chase away the image. "Thirsty, too," she added.

She must be dehydrated from standing in the hot Texas sun too long. It was the only explanation for her wayward thoughts concerning the man's mouth.

"Then let's go," he said. He easily lifted his son to his broad shoulders and started up the gentle rise to the house.

Hannah and her mother exchanged small talk as they walked arm in arm behind Dev. Hannah admired the long, easy stride of the man. The obvious close bond between father and son warmed her heart. She was curious about the woman Dev had married. And what had happened between the two that had left him alone raising his son.

A few minutes later they climbed up the steps of

Dev's imposing, two-story, white clapboard house with wraparound porch and overhang. The roofline was an interesting array of peaks, with a circular turret and balcony in front. She counted two chimneys that she could see and lots of decorative wood adorning the railing.

Her mother led the way into a large foyer with living room on one side, dining room on the other, each decorated with crown moulding and chair rails. Their footsteps rang on the distressed oak floor as they continued down the hall. Entering an enormous kitchen, she glanced around, noting the new-looking appliances, hunter-green granite countertops and cooktop range with oven below and built-in microwave above. Right across from it was a ceramic-tiled island with an overhang on the other side where four oak stools sat.

On the far side of the room in a nook complete with window seat, stood an oak table with ten matching ladderback chairs. Tasteful paper in a floral pattern hung on the bottom half of the walls while light beige paint contrasted beautifully with the white chair rail and decorative mouldings on the top half.

"This is charming," Hannah said, looking around in awe.

"Thanks. My folks redecorated about a year ago." Dev lifted Ben from his shoulders. "Go wash up, son."

"I already did, Dad."

"How long ago?" Dev rested his hands on lean hips as his son looked up at him with a slightly guilty look.

"In town," Ben answered vaguely.

"About four hours ago," Polly confirmed.

"Quit stalling, squirt."

"Okay," he grumbled, then disappeared down another hall.

"He's going to need some help reaching the sink," Polly said, as she set out cookies, milk, fruit and iced tea. "I'd send his father," she commented, giving the hunk hovering nearby a phony stern look, "but nine times out of ten more water winds up on the walls and floor than on their hands and faces."

"I'll go," Hannah offered. "I need to wash up, too."

"It's down that hall," Dev said. "If you see the utility room, you've gone too far."

"Thanks," she answered, and headed off after his son.

She found the room and saw Ben reaching without success to turn on the light. "Need some help, pal?"

"No." Ben shook his head. Then he looked at her and she realized how much he resembled his father. "Maybe a little."

She laughed and flipped the switch up with her thumb. The room was charming and functional. It had the same wood floor as the rest of the first story of the house. But the walls from top to bottom were covered with a tiny floral-print wallpaper, containing the same shades she'd seen in the kitchen. Wooden signs enhanced the country decor. The first that caught her eye read, So It Ain't Home Sweet Home. Adjust! Another advised, Thou Shalt Not Whine.

She smiled, then looked down at the small boy on tiptoe squirming this way and that to reach the spigot and soap pump. "Let me help," she said, squirting some into his grubby little hand and turning on the water. Lifting him with one arm around his middle, she used her free hand to wet his palms and rub the bubbles around as she chattered. "Your dad told me you'll be four next week. I bet you'll be able to reach the light switch then.''

He met her gaze in the mirror and grinned. ''Yes, I will.''

''You're a pretty big guy.''

He nodded and a lock of brown hair the same color as Dev's fell over his forehead. ''When I'm four, Daddy's going to give me a horse.''

''Wow. You're pretty brave. I'm afraid of horses.''

''Daddy's going to teach me to ride. If he showed you how, you wouldn't be a scaredy cat.''

Hannah was so taken with his utter confidence in Dev that she almost didn't mind the scaredy cat remark. Having never known that feeling toward her own father, she couldn't help envying the boy.

''If your dad put me on a horse, I'm not so sure I wouldn't be scared,'' she said. But she wasn't talking about the horse part.

''How about we find out?''

Dev's deep voice surprised her at the same time it raised goose bumps on her arms. She'd been so wrapped up in hand-washing and wondering about the things Ben's daddy could show her, she hadn't noticed the dad in question in the doorway behind her.

''Find out what?'' she asked, setting the child down and giving him the hand towel.

''Let's see if Ben's right and I can teach you not to be scared—on a horse.''

''Daddy *can* help you,'' Ben said with absolute confidence.

''How about tomorrow morning?'' Dev suggested, leaning against the doorjamb. ''Before it gets hot.''

It could be ten degrees below zero and if he was nearby she would be hot, Hannah thought. If she said no, she'd look like the world's biggest coward to a four-year-old. And she wasn't too keen on Dev thinking that of her either.

"Okay," she said, ruffling the boy's hair. She looked in the mirror, adjusting her gaze up to meet the tall cowboy's. "I'll meet you in the corral bright and early."

Maybe if it was bright enough and early enough, she would be brave enough to face Dev—and the horse.

Chapter Two

After a restless night, Dev had risen earlier than usual. He'd wanted to get work out of the way so he had plenty of time for Hannah's riding lesson. Except why he should go to so much trouble was what had kept him awake in the first place. Here on the ranch, there were always a million and one things to do. Not to mention the godawful paperwork he avoided as long as he possibly could. Given a choice between four walls and a computer spreadsheet program or outdoors and the horses, there was no contest.

All night long he hadn't been able to stop factoring Hannah Morgan into the outdoors and horses part. Because he'd thought her presence would be awkward and it wasn't. Because he couldn't take his eyes off her. Because he'd watched his son take a fancy to her. Because she'd implied that he'd been Destiny High's all-around playboy.

That's not the way he remembered it. She must have him confused with another cowboy she'd tutored.

But for those reasons and probably some he hadn't thought of yet, it was a fact that he now stood in the corral, horse saddled and waiting for her, at the time they'd agreed on. As if that wasn't bad enough, he was waiting with more anticipation than he wanted to feel. He hadn't seen Hannah yet today. He'd been out of the house and working before sunup, same as every other morning. Which was why he was so grateful to have Polly to look after Ben.

Was it gratitude that had goaded him into this offer to teach Hannah to ride? Her mother had bailed him out big time by taking care of the house and his son. Hannah had doctored Newy's bum shoulder yesterday. And Dev had to admit she'd impressed him with her skill. So he was beholden to both of the Morgan women. Was that enough to explain why the prospect of seeing Hannah had him lit up inside like the grand opening of a Las Vegas casino?

His memories of her in high school were hazy at best. He remembered the tutoring. How could he forget? It had been damned humiliating. His grades had been pretty good—in everything but physics. To maintain sports eligibility, he'd been forced to get help in that subject. His teacher had insisted it be Hannah, who was tops in her honors class. But not only was she several years younger, she was a *girl* and a brainer. At a time when he was struggling to be a man, she'd made him feel like a greenhorn kid.

She'd been skinny as a boy with glasses bigger than her face. Who knew in ten years she'd grow breasts and curves that would turn her into a package cute as could be? He'd never guessed that behind those Coke bottle lenses she'd had eyes bigger and bluer than a field of Texas bluebonnets.

And so what?

She was here for six weeks, to rest up and see her mother. The visit was nothing more than temporary because her life was on the west coast. He'd been burned once by a woman who'd believed greener pastures were anywhere but Destiny. Hannah had left for college earlier than most and carved out a life for herself fifteen hundred miles away. He would be a fool to let luscious curves and beautiful blue eyes make him forget that. His mission was to get her over her fear of horses. Then leave her be.

He glanced up the hill and saw her approaching. In her jeans, lime-green T-shirt and denim baseball hat, she looked awful darn tempting. She was covered from head to toe, but what she wore highlighted those mouthwatering curves he'd so recently thought about. His pulse kicked up a notch even though he could see very little of her flesh. That thought generated a subtle challenge inside him to see more.

She stopped at the fence separating them and looked up at the horse for a long moment before meeting his gaze. "Good morning."

He touched the brim of his hat. "Mornin'." He looked past her, expecting his son. The boy had taken quite a shine to her the day before. When he'd tucked Ben in last night, it was Hannah this, and Hannah that. He hadn't thought she would be able to leave the house without the little guy tagging along. Especially after he'd pleaded with her to go for it in the first place.

"Where's Ben?" he asked.

"He was listless when he got up this morning, and felt a little warm, so I took his temperature. It's a hundred and one."

"Do you think it's anything serious? Should I take him to—"

"Doc Holloway?" she asked, raising one eyebrow. "I actually graduated very near the top of my medical school class. Then I did a double residency in pediatrics and internal medicine. I could get a complex about you guys running to Doc Holloway when an honest-to-goodness doctor is within spitting distance."

"Sorry. I forgot." It probably had something to do with the fact that every time he laid eyes on her, he felt like he'd been kicked in the head by his favorite horse. That didn't exactly help a cowboy put his best boot forward. "Did you check him over?"

She nodded. "I always have my medical bag with me. Ears and throat looked okay. His chest sounded clear. At this point, there's nothing to treat. Some kids just run a temp when they get run down. Mom knows what to do for the symptoms—rest, meds to control the fever, and lots of fluids. He was keeping a low profile when I left the house."

"The Texas tornado? That's a miracle."

She laughed, showing straight white teeth and a world-class smile. Before he could stop himself, he thought that she should do it more often. His next thought—why should he care if she did?

She stepped up on the first rung of the fence. "Since your son didn't argue with the diagnosis and treatment, I figure it's probably what he needs."

"You're the doc."

"You finally remembered."

He looked down as he shuffled his boots in the dirt. "You make it hard for a man to forget."

"Sorry. It's gotten to be a habit I guess, because of my medical training. Speaking of which, Ben was pretty vocal about not wanting to drink so much. I suggested that soda was a good fluid to push. That put a sparkle in his eyes.''

"Pretty smart," he said. "But you always were."

"Yeah."

Her smile dimmed a shade at his remark and he wondered why. "Since Ben's in good hands with your mom, what do you say you put yourself in mine? In a manner of speaking."

The porcelain-smooth skin on her cheeks flushed pink. He hadn't intended that as a double entendre. But now that he thought about it, touching her wouldn't be too hard to take—if the parts of her that saw daylight were half as soft as the parts of her he'd been imagining that didn't.

"Have you ever heard the expression 'like father, like son'?"

He nodded. "Why?"

"Because you've got the same gleam in your eyes that I saw in Ben's. Somehow I don't think yours has anything to do with soda. So I have to assume it's role reversal."

"You lost me," he said, shaking his head.

"Now you're the teacher and I'm the student."

"Ah." He couldn't suppress a grin.

She raised one eyebrow. "You wouldn't hold that against me, would you?"

"You mean that whole dictator thing you had going on in high school?" He shook his head. "It never entered my mind."

"Then why are you smiling like that?"

"Me?" he said, pointing to his chest. "I'm not grinnin' like the price of beef went sky-high. I never smile."

She looked warily at the animal waiting patiently beside him. "I don't have to get on that horse, you know."

Dev glanced at the gelding. "You mean Trouble? Why he's as gentle as they come."

"Then why is he named Trouble?" she shot back.

He shrugged. "Seemed to fit. He was sickly from the day he was born. Took a lot of nursemaiding. But he grew up big and strong. Didn't you, boy?" he said, patting the horse's neck.

"I have a bad feeling about this—"

Something deep down inside Dev said don't let her back out. Don't let her walk away now. "Look, Hannah, I could shame you into this. The words yellow, coward and chicken come to mind. But I won't stoop to name-calling."

"Thank goodness," she said wryly.

"Unless you force me to."

"Okay. Challenge noted and desired response achieved," she said, climbing over the fence.

He noticed that she kept him between herself and the horse. Then her eyes grew bigger and bluer as she stared up at the big, gentle gelding.

"We can ride double until you feel comfortable," he offered.

"What makes you think riding with you would make me more comfortable?" she asked, looking at him.

He hadn't thought her eyes could get any bigger or more beautiful, but they did. And he had a feeling when she was talking uncomfortable, it had more to do with him than the horse. Why that should make him feel like grinning, he couldn't say. The fact was—he wanted to, but of course he didn't.

"I'll ride behind you till you get the feel of it up

there. Till you're not as jumpy as spit on a hot skillet,"
he added.

"I haven't heard that one since I left Texas."

"You ready to give it a go?" he asked.

She caught the corner of her full bottom lip between
her teeth as she looked from him to the horse then over
her shoulder to the house as if she wanted to take off
at a dead run. Finally, she met his gaze and straightened her spine. "Okay. Never let it be said that Hannah
Morgan, M.D., is not full of gumption and grit."

There was the girl from Destiny that he remembered.
For just an instant he'd heard the Texas drawl back in
her voice. The snappy, husky, seductive tone turned his
thoughts to things he couldn't do on a horse. Well, he
could, but it would be damned stupid, and pretty uncomfortable.

Whoa. Down boy, he thought. Rein in that idea
pronto. This was a friendly lesson. He only wanted to
teach her to ride, as a favor to her mom. The least he
could do was pay some attention to Polly's daughter
during her visit, to show her a good time.

Is that why it seemed so important to get up close
and personal? Just a good time? For her or him? Not
to mention that there were lots of ways to make her
feel easy on a horse without riding double.

Ignoring that sensible thought, he said, "Lesson
number one—you need to make nice with Trouble."

"I think I've already done that. Just by showing
up," she said. Hesitantly, she sidled up beside him.

He looked at her and wondered who she thought
she'd made nice with—the horse or him. "Not even
close," he answered. It was safer not to make it about
him. "You've got to touch Trouble. Like this," he said

taking her right hand and placing it on the animal's neck.

Her wrist was delicate, fragile. She was small, barely came up to his shoulder. Something stretched inside him. If he didn't know better, he would think it was his protective streak stirring to life. But he *did* know better. Corie had stomped it right out of him. She'd told him over and over: in this day and age, women wanted a lot out of life. Being a wife and mother wasn't everything. She didn't need a man to define who she was or protect her. His ex-wife's putting her money where her mouth was and leaving had hit him like a truck and Dev had gotten the message loud, clear and painful. He could stand back and let Hannah do her thing just fine, thank you very much.

But he stood behind her, close enough that he could smell the fragrance of her—something floral and sassy mixed with soap. Her blond hair was tucked through the opening in the back of her hat and trailed down, skimming her shoulder blades. He wanted to free the silken strands and run his hands through them. Warmth radiated through him and sweat popped out on his forehead. So much for giving her an early lesson before it got hot.

"What do I do now?" she asked, glancing over her shoulder and up at him.

He swallowed—hard. "Just what you're doing. Let him get used to you." And me too, he thought. Damn that rusty tone in his voice. With any luck, she was too preoccupied with Trouble to notice.

"I think it's more like me getting used to him," she said nervously. "After all, he's bigger than me. By a lot."

So was Dev. A fact that fueled his pesky, persistent,

protective streak. "I won't let him hurt you," he promised.

It was on the tip of his tongue to add that he would never let anything hurt her. But he held back. A fact for which he was really grateful. He didn't want another woman in his life. Especially a career woman like Hannah.

"I appreciate that. Although if he takes it into his head to pulverize me, I'm not exactly sure how you could stop him."

"Even if something spooks him, usually there's warning. Time to get out of the way. There are signs. Restlessness. Shifting. Snorting. Same things that happen to you and me when we get rattled," he said.

"God knows *I* snort when I get riled up," she said.

"And here I thought you were brighter than the average bear. How intelligent is it to smart-mouth your tutor?"

"You tell me. I learned from you."

"I don't remember that."

"Selective memory. It's a condition that affects a lot of men," she added.

"Male bashing is not the best way to win friends and favorably influence your riding teacher. But I'm going to take the moral high ground and not hold it against you. Right now Trouble is just standing there as peaceful as you please."

"I'll ignore the contradiction in terms of that last statement," she said as she continued to stroke the horse's neck.

For several minutes, he just let her do that while the slender, delicate, elegant, smooth curve of her neck tortured him with wondering what that spot would taste like.

Good God Almighty! What in the world had gotten into him? This—whatever it was—was just plain nuts. The sooner he got her on a horse and fulfilled his fool's promise, the better. He'd just learned another lesson from Hannah. Don't be too quick to offer a riding lesson to a pretty, big-city, lady doctor.

"Okay," he said abruptly. "I think it's time to climb up on Trouble and see how it feels."

"I'm as ready as I'll ever be." She hesitated for a moment, her hand resting on the horse's neck. "What do I do?"

"One hand on the horn, left foot in the stirrup and haul yourself up, swinging the right over his rump. Easy as falling off a log."

She slid him a look over her shoulder. "No form of the word 'fall' should be spoken in this conversation."

"My mistake." He held back his grin until she glanced away.

"Mistake is another word I don't want to hear."

"How about 'just do it'?"

"Words to live by," she said, but her voice was tight.

She followed his instructions and hauled herself up a little awkwardly. As badly as he wanted to put his hands on her waist and help, he kept his arms at his sides. In spite of the fact that she was stiff as last Sunday's corn bread. Apprehension was written all over her, from the tense shoulders down to her shapely little fanny.

"Everything's fine, Hannah," he said, trying to reassure her.

"You're not leaving me up here by myself, are you?" she asked from her perch in the saddle.

He wanted to. But he was the one who'd started this.

His daddy hadn't raised a quitter. Next time, he'd be more careful not to let his mouth write checks that his body would be foolish to cash.

"Nope."

He took her small, sneakered foot out of the stirrup and stuck his boot in. Holding onto the horn, he swung up onto the horse's rump, letting her have the saddle all to herself. He successfully fought the urge to put both arms around her. But with his chest to her back, he could feel her shaking. In spite of all his warnings, his hands went to her waist, just to steady her he told himself.

"Relax," he said, close to her ear, stirring the wisps of golden hair that had slid out from her hat.

She shivered and he assumed it was from fear, since Texas wasn't even close to cool this time of year. It surely didn't have anything to do with him and the fact that they were as close as two peas in a pod.

"Relax," she repeated, as if she were memorizing physics properties. "Focus."

He picked up the looped reins he'd rested around the saddle horn, then held them out. "These are connected to the bit in his mouth. Pull on the right to make him go that way. Left turns him in that direction. Grip with your knees to keep from bouncing. Your backside will thank you later."

"You make it sound easy enough," she said. "I think I've got the hang of it. That's probably enough for today. All that information is just buzzing around in my head. My mind is fairly spinning." She glanced at him over her shoulder. "Wouldn't want to overdo it."

"Lucky for you I'm here."

"Why lucky? Aside from the fact that if he throws us, you'll go first to cushion my fall."

"Because you can't get down unless I do. And I don't plan on it until I know you're not going to give up on this."

"I don't understand why that's so important to you."

He shrugged, beyond trying to come up with a reasonable answer, even for himself. To her he said, "Because it's a damn shame that a girl born and raised in Destiny, Texas, is afraid of a horse. You'll give the town a bad name."

"If it's any consolation, I wasn't raised here very long. I left for college when I was sixteen."

"Doesn't matter. You've got Texas in your blood. And the least you can do is take a spin around this corral before you head for the hills. Humor me."

"Okay." They sat there for a few moments before she asked, "How do I make him go?"

"Gentle pressure with your knees. It wouldn't hurt to talk to him."

She nodded. "Go, Trouble," she said hesitantly at the same time as she followed his instructions. The horse moved forward slowly and began to walk around the corral. "It worked."

"Don't sound so surprised. I'm a good teacher."

"And humble too."

After several turns around the enclosure, he felt her begin to loosen up. It was time for her to go it alone, but that meant he had to get off. Everything inside him balked at the thought.

But before he could decide what to do, he heard his son calling. "Daddy. Hannah."

Instantly, Dev covered both of Hannah's hands with

his own, helping her bring the horse to a standstill. Then he slid off Trouble's rump. He reached up and lifted her down before walking to the fence. Ben got there at the same time, huffing and puffing from running.

"Daddy, hurry."

"What's wrong? How are you feeling?"

"Polly said my tem-pitcher's better. But you gotta come quick. Hannah, too. She's a doctor. She'll know what to do." Then he turned and raced away, in the direction of the house.

Hannah instantly went into doctor mode. Was there something wrong with her mother? In two seconds she was at the gate opening it.

"Mom," was the only word she could get out when she looked at Dev.

He nodded. "I'm right behind you."

Hannah hadn't known she could move that fast. She'd handled emergencies during her training, but it had never involved a family member. She loved her mother so much. The woman had made more sacrifices for her than she could count. Hannah was almost where she'd worked so hard to be—almost in a position to give Polly the easy life. If anything happened to her...

It seemed to take forever, but several minutes later she burst through the kitchen door. "Mom?"

"Here, honey," the familiar voice said. "In the utility room."

Hannah raced past the island to the hallway and the door on her left. Her mother smiled at her, then down at Ben who was crouched by a box. Relief flooded her that there was nothing wrong with Polly. Then she inspected the box more closely and saw the cat in it. A moment later, she realized what was happening.

With a wide-eyed, worried expression, Ben looked up at her. "Callie's havin' babies. She needs a doctor."

Hannah nodded solemnly. He was too young to understand that the cat would probably do fine on her own. If not, she needed a vet. But she said, "I'll get my medical bag."

She hurried into the family room and retrieved the bag from where she'd left it after examining the boy earlier. When she returned, there was a new arrival. Dev was crouched beside his son, staring at the newest tiny bundle of slick fur.

"Where's Mom?" she asked.

"She said she had things to do and since reinforcements had arrived, she went upstairs."

Hannah nodded, then took a paper-wrapped package of disposable gloves from her kit and put them on. Then she knelt on Ben's other side. Reaching in, she carefully picked up the brand-new kitten then nestled it where Callie could reach if she wanted to clean it up.

A few minutes later, there was another teeny-weeny furball, and she put it beside the first. After about forty-five minutes, three more little ones had arrived.

Hannah rubbed a hand over the mother cat's side. "I think that's the last one," she said.

Ben's brown eyes were bright as he looked at her. "Wow, five babies. You're the best doctor in the whole world."

"I didn't do anything," she said truthfully. "Callie did all the work."

The little boy shook his head as he stood. He threw himself into her arms. "I want you to stay here forever, Hannah."

Chapter Three

Still squatting beside the mother cat's birthing box, Hannah steadied herself from Ben's enthusiastic embrace. Over the boy's head, Hannah met Dev's gaze. He was so close she could see flecks of gold that made his brown eyes almost hazel. Or maybe it was the fear she saw that made them seem different. In her line of work, all too often she saw parental anxiety and recognized it in Dev now. And she thought she knew the reason for his apprehension.

"Wow," she said, rubbing the boy's sturdy little back. Gently, she pulled his arms from around her neck. "Forever is a really long time, pal."

Dev was still hunkered down beside her. He put his big hand on the boy's shoulder and protectively tugged him back between his jeans-clad thighs. Then he pulled Ben just a little closer until the child's back rested against his wide chest and wrapped his forearms around the boy's middle. "Hannah lives in California, son."

Bingo. Dev *was* worried, about his son pinning any hopes on her staying. She'd taken an oath to help, not hurt people, and that included little boys with big crushes. She needed to set him straight.

She nodded. "Your dad's right, Ben. I just came to Texas for a visit."

"Does visit mean you can't move here?"

She looked into the little guy's sweet, earnest face, then the father's tight, tense features. Oh, boy. She'd been there less than twenty-four hours and she felt like she was dodging two Texas tornadoes—father and son.

She shook her head. "No, but visit means that I'm only here for a short time and then I have to go back home."

Trustingly, Ben patted his father's big hand where it rested against his abdomen. "So you *can* move here," he said, his four-year-old logic simplifying everything.

"It's not that easy, son."

"Why?" The little guy turned puppy dog eyes on his dad.

"Because Hannah's things are there and—"

The boy half turned and put an arm around his father's neck. "I know what. How 'bout if we help? We'll put all her stuff in your truck and bring it here."

"Oh, sweetie—" His words squeezed Hannah's heart. This pint-sized cowboy could grow on her without half trying.

Dev met her gaze and along with his fear she saw the tiniest bit of humor. "I should get out the map and show him how far it is. But somehow I still don't think he would get it."

She smiled. "Yeah, kids are pretty literal."

"I do get it, Daddy. I want Hannah to stay and we should help her."

Dev curved one hand around the boy's small shoulders and turned him so they were face to face. "Hannah is a busy lady, an important doctor. She lives in California and her job is there."

"Makin' people better?"

"That's right." Dev nodded encouragingly.

"Kids get sick here, too," the child pointed out sagely.

Oh, boy, she thought. Ben Hart, almost four—and pretty precocious for his age—could rip her heart out with one chubby little fist and walk away with it in his back pocket.

"Yes, they do," she said. "And then you go to see Doc Holloway. He was my doctor when I was a little girl."

Dev glanced at her, then back to his son. "You know how I work hard to make the ranch grow?" When the child nodded, he continued, "Hannah has worked hard like that to join a practice in California."

"But she's already a doctor. Why does she hafta practice?"

She caught her top lip between her teeth to stop the laugh that threatened. "A practice is a doctor's business, like raising horses and cattle is your daddy's job," she explained.

"So bring your business here," Ben said.

"Oh, sweetie. I can't." She searched desperately for the words to make him understand. "Could your daddy move his ranch somewhere else?"

From the safe circle of his father's arms, the child half turned toward her and she could almost see the wheels turning in his mind. Finally, he shook his head. "Nope."

"It's the same way with my business. My patients

are a long way away. If I live here in Texas, they can't come see me to make them better. I have to stay there.''

"But *I'm* here," he said, pointing a finger at his small chest.

Oh, mercy, she thought. "Yes, you are here. And I'm going to be very sad when I have to leave you.''

"Don't leave," the boy said, as if that settled everything. "Then Daddy and I can make you happy.''

Dev coughed uncomfortably. "Her dreams aren't here, son.''

The boy's brow furrowed as he thought that one over. "How come, Daddy? When I have a bad dream it's here too.''

"I'm not talking about nightmares," Dev explained patiently. "I'm talking about what Hannah wants in her life. And she doesn't want a life here. A man can't make a woman happy if her dreams don't include him.''

Hannah saw the faraway look in his eyes and the flash of pain. Was he talking about his ex-wife, Ben's mother? Again she wondered what had split them up. What was his story?

Ben concentrated on his father's words for a while, then said, "I know. We hafta change Hannah's dream to 'clude us, Daddy.''

Dev's mouth curved up at the corners and again she couldn't help wondering what his lips would feel like against her own. Heat started in her breasts and radiated north and south. If the warmth showed pink in her cheeks, she hoped he would chalk it up to their time outdoors. In a way that was true although not because of the sun. Sitting so close to him on that horse had given her trouble of the man/woman kind.

"One person can't change another person's dreams, son," Dev explained patiently. "Hannah has already made up her own mind what she wants to do."

"You hafta change her mind." It was as if his father hadn't spoken.

Hannah wondered if the child had inherited that stubborn, single-minded determination from his father. If so, and Dev turned the force of it on her, there could be hell to pay. But that wasn't likely. This was history repeating itself. She'd noticed him, but he wouldn't give her a tumble.

"I can't change her mind," Dev said.

More like he didn't want to, Hannah realized. That was a relief. But the thought rang just a bit hollow.

"Sure you can, Daddy. You tell me all the time I can do anything if I just try. You gotta try." His eyes, the same shade as his father's, lit up. "I know what you can do."

"I know I'm going to regret this," Dev said to Hannah. Then he looked at Ben. "What can I do?"

"Kiss Hannah." The child nodded emphatically.

The heat that had just receded returned to Hannah's cheeks. "Sweetie, I don't think your dad wants to do that."

"Sure he does. He kissed Cassie Gordon once and he did it good because I heard him tell Polly that she wouldn't leave him alone afterward."

Her mouth twitched at the look on Dev's face. He was still wearing his hat. The shadow it cast prevented her from seeing if he blushed, but he was definitely squirming. Chalk one up for the offspring.

"Is this true?" she asked.

"Well—"

"So you're still the Pied Piper of Destiny's female population?"

"Not even close."

"But what about poor Cassie Gordon?"

"Don't you worry your pretty little head over her," Dev said wryly. "She's a barracuda in sheep's clothing."

"That's a mixed metaphor."

"Since when is English grammar your specialty?"

She shrugged. "I'm an all-around gifted gal."

Ben put his little hands on his father's face and turned it toward him. "Daddy, you hafta kiss Hannah. You can change her dream. It works in the movies."

"What are you letting this child watch?" she asked.

He rubbed a hand across the back of his neck. "That's a good question."

"I saw it in *Cinderella, Sleeping Beauty, Snow White*— all of 'em. Polly said they're okay."

"You're going to have your hands full with him, Dev. He's a bright one. If anyone knows what a double-edged sword that can be, it's me."

He sighed, then looked at Ben. "Life isn't as easy as a movie or a book—or high school," he said meeting her gaze.

"High school easy? I prefer to think of it as the school of hard knocks," she said.

"But Daddy—"

"Ben," he said firmly, "this discussion is over. Hannah and I are going in the kitchen. You watch the cat clean up her babies. And don't touch them," he warned. "Mothers will do anything to protect their babies and she might scratch you if she's afraid you'll hurt them."

"Mothers do that?" Ben asked.

''Yeah,'' Dev said. ''Except yours,'' he added, too softly for the preoccupied boy to hear.

He pushed to his feet, then held a hand down to Hannah. She took it, letting him help her up. As surely as she felt the warmth of his palm enveloping hers, she felt Dev's concern for his child. Whatever he asked, she would do. If it meant not hurting Ben, she was prepared to leave the ranch.

After dinner and the dreaded paperwork, Dev walked out on the front porch to clear his head. He stretched as he stared at the clear Texas sky sprinkled with thousands of twinkling stars. Was there a prettier sight anywhere? He doubted it. Unless it was the way the sun brought out the gold in Hannah's hair.

Good Lord. She'd been there twenty-four hours and he couldn't seem to control his thoughts about her. Especially her full, sensuous lips—a mouth made for kissing.

He recalled telling Ben that life wasn't as simple as movies or books—or high school. Hannah remembered it as the school of hard knocks. But he disagreed. Back then, it was a whole lot easier to ignore Hannah. He'd never once thought about what it would feel like to kiss her. Since seeing her again, he'd thought of very little else. Now that was a hard knock.

As the refreshing evening breeze washed over his heated skin, he took a deep breath. His gaze wandered over the front yard and the outbuildings in the distance. As it swung in closer, he thought he saw movement in the white-painted gazebo that sat about a hundred yards from the house. Looking closer, he spotted a lime-green shirt.

Hannah.

She'd disappeared as soon as she'd helped Polly clean up the dinner dishes. If she was trying to hide, she'd have to do better than neon green. He was a fool three times over for even considering it, but decided it would be less than Texas neighborly to ignore her. He walked down the steps and crossed the length of the sidewalk, then into the shadowed interior of the small, intimate structure.

"Evening," he said.

"Hi."

"Mind if I join you?"

"Nope."

He sat down in a spot he gauged to be a safe distance across from her. Unfortunately she was upwind. A sweet, flowery, feminine fragrance he somehow knew he would always connect to Hannah drifted to him on the breeze. Her hair was loose and caught behind her ears, held there by a headband that matched her shirt. The moonlight turned the silky strands to silver. Sitting ramrod straight, she held her knees together, hands on her slender thighs. Her eyes looked enormous in the soft, romantic light.

"Pretty…" he said.

"Hmm?"

He cleared his throat. "Pretty night."

"Mmm," was her only comment.

He leaned back against the wood enclosure and stretched his arms out, resting them on the railing. "That was a great dinner. Your mom is a good cook."

"Yes, she is. When I was growing up, she stretched the grocery budget as far as it would go and came up with some truly imaginative meals." She smiled, a faraway expression on her face. "Clean out the refrigerator for two, hamburger surprise. The surprise was no hamburger anywhere in the meal.''

"You had a rough time growing up?" It didn't seem she could sit any straighter, but she tensed at his words.

"We got by," was all she said.

"Do you like to cook?"

As soon as the words were out of his mouth, Dev wanted to call them back. After what Ben had said earlier, it sounded way too much like a job interview.

"Me? Cook?" She laughed and the musical sound burrowed inside him. "You have no idea how funny that is."

"A simple no would do."

"It's not that easy. I believe anyone who can read can follow directions and put together a meal. Then there are people like Mom who can take a recipe and make magic. I would rather read the latest medical journal."

"So you made the right choice—becoming a doctor?"

"No question about it."

The words were filled with satisfaction and passion, he thought, for her work. He couldn't help wondering if any man could coax that reaction from her. A man like him.

Foolish thought number one. A man like him didn't want to coax any kind of reaction from a woman like her. She'd just admitted her devotion to her work and the fact that she wasn't the homemaker type. Did he need a rude awakening with a two-by-four to get that message through his thick skull? He'd made one mistake. He wasn't about to walk into another with his eyes wide open. Especially with Ben to protect.

"Can I ask you something, Dev? You left the house

after the kittens were born and I didn't get a chance to talk to you.''

"Sure.'' Please. Anything to get his mind off her.

"Is it all right with you that I'm here?''

Hell, yeah, was his instant thought. He tamped it down before answering. "Why would you ask?''

She linked her fingers together and he suspected if he could see them, he would find that her knuckles were white.

"Because of Ben.''

He leaned forward, resting his forearms on his thighs. He let his linked hands dangle between his splayed knees. His son was his reason for everything.

"What about Ben?'' The words came out more sharply than he intended.

"I saw the look on your face earlier, when he said he didn't want me to go.''

"He's only three.''

"Four next week,'' she pointed out.

"Yeah. You said he's bright. Maybe in a week he'll understand how far away California is and why you can't stay.''

"Maybe. But I'm concerned about his unreasonable expectations.''

"About?''

"Us,'' she said.

"Because?''

"You don't want a serious relationship anymore than I do.''

"Really?'' he asked.

Since when did telling him what he did or didn't want fall under the heading of medical advice? It didn't make any difference that she'd guessed right. Or was he annoyed because she confirmed his suspicion that she wasn't interested? "So your medical expertise is in the mental health field? Or you're psychic?"

"I've got twenty/twenty vision with my contacts and I saw your face when you explained to Ben that a man can't make a woman happy if her dreams don't include him."

"I just don't want the boy to get hurt."

"I've dedicated my life to making people better. I wouldn't hurt him."

"Not intentionally." He let out a long breath. "And yeah. You're right. I don't want him to get ideas about anything, you know, between you and I."

"What happened with you and Ben's mother?"

"The usual. Irreconcilable differences."

"Two multiple syllable words that don't tell me a thing. What's your story, Dev?"

"Since when does a doctor need the gory, personal details?"

"You'd be surprised. Each patient is a mystery and the symptoms are clues. One tiny fact if overlooked can cause a doctor to make a wrong diagnosis. And a person's mental state can have a major impact on recovery."

"I'm recovered just fine," he snapped.

"Okay. Then call me a curious old friend who's wondering what you've been up to for the last ten years."

For reasons he didn't understand, he wanted to tell Hannah what happened. For Ben's sake, he decided. "Corie was beautiful—probably still is," he said with a chuckle that lacked humor. "She was the rodeo queen."

"Lucky her," she said, a wistful note in her voice. Something in her tone made him defensive. Probably her comment about adoring females following him around. When was she going to give him credit for ten years of growing up?

"Believe it or not, there's more criteria to being chosen queen than just looks. Although she had looks and then some."

"I believe you."

"Girls have to have good grades—"

"Wow. I could have been in the running."

"And involved in their school and community. It's a big commitment on top of being pretty."

"Well, if pretty is involved in any way, that lets me out."

"You underestimate yourself," he said, his voice gruff.

She looked down at her hands in her lap. "You were telling me about you and Corie."

"Right," he said, relieved to go back to anything besides Hannah. "I wanted what I grew up with—a family, a stay-at-home woman who would be there at night for me and our children. I thought she felt the same way I did. I fell hard and fast for the rodeo queen."

"So you married her."

"Yeah."

"What happened?"

"She got pregnant right away and Ben was born. But all her life, everyone told her she was pretty enough to be a New York model. She couldn't get that out of her head."

"I know what it's like to have a dream," she said gently.

"Yeah. Well she did, all right. She worked hard and got back into shape real fast. I didn't realize her dream was an obsession until she told me she was leaving. She had to try."

"What did you do?"

"I tried to talk her out of it. Then I just tried to convince her not to go until Ben was a little older."

"She wanted to take Ben with her?"

He shook his head. "And to this day I can't decide if that makes it better or worse." He shrugged. "In the end, neither Ben nor I was enough to keep her on the ranch."

For him, the sting was gone from her leaving. But he was left with the lesson that career and family were like oil and water. Now he was solely responsible for protecting his son.

"Does she see Ben?"

"Not really. She's busy. Part of me wishes she'd fallen flat on her fanny. But she's getting steady work—not the pie-in-the-sky stuff, but she keeps a roof over her head and food on the table and sometimes she even remembers to send him something for Christmas and his birthday."

"I'm sorry, Dev."

"It doesn't matter."

"Don't spout macho bull. Of course it does or you wouldn't have tried to protect Ben from me."

"I didn't—"

She held her hands up. "That wasn't a criticism. Just a fact. I like that you did. You'd be surprised how many parents don't care about their children. He's lucky to have you for a father."

Somehow, her words took a heavy weight from his shoulders. "Thank you, ma'am."

"You're welcome. Now the question is finding him a mother."

"The answer is—not in this lifetime."

An unladylike noise that sounded an awful lot like a snort came at him from across the gazebo. "More bull," she said. "But what can you expect from a man whose life's work is raising stock."

"Is that sass? And humor? Did you just make a pun?"

She laughed. "I reckon so."

"Okay. Just checking."

"Seriously, Dev, Destiny is probably the best place to find a woman who wants the same things you do."

In a pig's eye, he thought. No one had gotten his attention. Correction, no one until he'd seen Hannah again. A woman who lived fifteen hundred miles away. How perverse was that?

"I'm not looking," was all he said.

"It can't hurt that women always follow you around like the Pied Piper," she said, ignoring his protest.

"Says who?"

"Says me."

"You must be thinking of another cowboy."

She shook her head. "I don't think so. At least that's the way it was in high school."

"Times change."

"What about Cassie Gordon?"

"Ben doesn't always get his facts straight."

"So you didn't kiss her?"

"I didn't say that."

"But her kiss didn't make the earth move? Didn't make you see stars, or hear bells and banjoes?"

"Good Lord, Hannah. Tell me you haven't been reading those women's magazines instead of your medical journals."

"It doesn't matter where I got my information. I've heard when it's good you see fireworks."

"They're not talking about kissing," he said wryly. "Have you ever seen fireworks?"

"We were talking about you," she answered with a neat little sidestep. "Maybe your ideal woman doesn't exist."

"Why would you say that?"

"It's a new millennium. Women have careers in addition to families."

"When two salaries are necessary to put food on the table and make ends meet, I can see it."

"That's not always how it is. Women have hopes and dreams and aspirations. And believe it or not—brains."

"Okay. But it's not especially bright to get involved with someone who doesn't want the same things I do. I'm not stupid, Hannah."

"I never said you were. I always thought you were smart."

"Until Corie. I thought she wanted what I did. I found out I was wrong. But I won't make the same mistake twice. I won't ever again get involved with someone who's not on the same page as me. I'll do anything to prevent my son from being hurt again."

At the mention of his son, Dev glanced to the boy's upstairs window on the front of the house. He saw a small face peeking out at them and wondered how long Ben had been watching. And hoping to see evidence of them being a couple, he expected.

"I wouldn't hurt him, Dev. I'm serious about that. I could find a place to stay in town—"

"No way. I couldn't ask you to do that. For two very good reasons."

"Such as?" she asked.

"Number one, I owe your mother more than I can ever repay. Besides the fact that we already established how much I appreciate her cooking skills, she's great with Ben. I'd be lost without her. And she's been looking forward to this visit for too long and wants to spend every moment she can with you."

"I've been looking forward to it too," she admitted. "So what's number two?"

"How would it look breaking hospitality rule number one of the Texas gentleman's cowboy code of the west? A gracious host would never send a lady packing." He shook his head. "Just isn't done."

She laughed. "Okay. But there must be something we can do to convince Ben not to get his hopes up."

"Actually there is. I have an idea."

"I thought I smelled something burning." The corners of her mouth turned up.

"Very funny," he said. Although the heat her smile produced inside him wasn't funny at all.

"Sorry. So how are you going to convince the little matchmaker that I'm medical, you're country western and never the twain shall meet—or something like that?"

"There's one thing that might do it."

"What's that?"

"A kiss."

Chapter Four

Hannah's heart started to pound. "Excuse me? I thought you said kiss."

"You heard right. How about it?"

She was glad there was a large span between them. If he hadn't been sitting on the opposite side of the gazebo, she might feel compelled to stand and relocate to another county. But he was a safe distance away. So she casually settled herself on the wooden bench attached to the railing, leaning back against it as she folded her arms across her chest.

"Did I miss something here?" she asked. "I was under the impression you wanted to convince your son that there was nothing between us and unlikely to ever *be* anything. I'm not quite sure I understand what a kiss would accomplish."

"Ben needs a reality check. He thinks life is like the movies. One kiss and everyone lives happily ever after."

"Like the fairy tales," she said.

He nodded. "A kiss brings the princess out of her coma."

"Yeah." She couldn't help smiling. "Or turns the toad into a prince."

"I believe it was a frog," he said wryly. "But you heard him as well as I did. Basically he's convinced that your dreams can be changed by a single kiss."

"You know, Dev, I've lived in California. I'm not a little girl from Hickville, Texas, anymore."

"What does that mean?"

"Why in the world would you expect me to believe this song and dance that a kiss will help Ben get the message?"

"Because I believe in teaching with visual aids?"

She couldn't see it but his amused tone told her there was a twinkle in his eyes. She'd only been there a short time, but that sexy expression was branded forever into her memory. Maybe she *should* leave the ranch—and not just for Ben's sake. For her own.

"So you have no ulterior motive?" she questioned.

He put his hand over his heart. "May lightning strike me if I'm not telling the truth. The fact that you are a beautiful woman has absolutely nothing to do with my motivation."

"Let me make sure I understand. If I was so homely I had to sneak up on a glass of water, you would still want to do it?" The words evoked past humiliation. It was diluted, but still there. She'd once overheard him saying that about her to a group of his friends including Mitch Rafferty, Jack Riley and Grady O'Connor. She hadn't forgotten. Would he remember?

"If you had a hump on your back and a wart on your nose, I would still be asking permission to kiss you."

"I don't believe you for a minute," she scoffed.

"You're a beautiful woman, Hannah. So there's no way for me to prove I'm telling the truth."

Oh mercy! The world champion charmer was turning the flattery on full blast. God help her, it was working. She didn't for a single moment believe that he believed she was pretty. But she was beginning to want very much to kiss him.

She cleared her throat. "Not that I agree with this crazy idea, but if I—If we…kiss, how will Ben know? Do you want me to swear on a stack of bibles and sign an affidavit in blood?"

He laughed. "Nothing so dramatic or painful. Don't look now, but he's spying on us from his bedroom window over yonder. We can take care of this right now."

"Yeah?"

Dev nodded. "It will teach him that a kiss isn't a life-altering experience. He'll also get the message that in spite of it, when your time here is up, you'll go back to your work in California."

"Whatever that might be, as in which prestigious medical practice in L.A. offers me the job of my dreams in pediatrics."

"Specifics aren't required for purposes of this kiss."

"Of course not."

She hadn't thought her heart could pound any harder, but hammer it did. Her adrenaline kicked in faster than an IV push of meds. The space in the gazebo seemed to shrink. Staring across it, she could see him in the moonlight. He looked relaxed. His hat was missing and she could see his brown hair, mussed as if he'd run his fingers through it countless times. The sleeves of his long-sleeved white shirt were rolled to just below his elbows and his worn jeans stretched across his thighs, outlining the muscles there. His mouth curved up. She wished she had a nickel for how many times in the last twenty-four hours she'd wondered what it would feel like to kiss him. Never again would she have to worry about money. And he was handing her the opportunity on a silver platter.

"You're not afraid, are you?" His tone was subtly challenging and his teeth flashed white with a sudden grin.

The combination made him look nearly irresistible.

But resist him she must. And yes, she was afraid. But to him she said, "Don't be ridiculous."

However unlikely that serious sparks would fly between them, it was still pointless to start something. There was no way she could finish it. She had to leave. The job she was hoping for would give her the income she needed to help her mother and pay her back for all the years of sacrifice. Not only that, there was a part of Hannah hyper-aware that Dev could be dangerous to her emotionally. There was no way she could stay in Destiny and she didn't intend to go back to California with a fractured heart.

No way would she be another romantic notch on Dev Hart's belt. Only she had a bad feeling that she'd judged him harshly. He'd been young and it was past time to get over the comments of the immature boy he'd been. But she couldn't seem to let go of one high school regret: she'd never gotten Dev's positive attention for anything but her brains. She had wondered from time to time in the last ten years what it would be like if he noticed her as a woman. In her wildest dreams, she'd never expected fantasy fulfillment. If only he'd gone bald and soft in all this time. But she wasn't that lucky. Not only had he gotten older, he'd gotten better. The idea made her shiver.

"Are you cold?" he asked.

How had he seen that? Was he a superhero? Did he have X-ray vision? She shook her head, unwilling to feed his ego by confessing the involuntary movement was all about him and the effect on her that she couldn't seem to stifle.

"It's a beautiful night," she said.

A perfect setting for a kiss. Damn him for suggesting it. And his reason, at least on the surface, was noble— to show his son that he couldn't always expect to get what he wanted. How endearing was that?

"So what do you say?" Dev asked. "He's spying on us. Shall we give him a taste of his own medicine?"

She wanted to tell him not in this lifetime. But Dev was not the dimmest bulb in the chandelier. He was brighter than the average bear and curious to boot. If she refused his suggestion, he would want to know why.

"If your remedy has any chance of working," she said, stalling, "it should look convincing. He's only four, but in my experience, kids are hard to fool."

"Medical school and a residency in pediatrics taught you that?"

"So I'm an overachiever," she said, teasing back. "How do we do it?"

"I could draw you a diagram," he said, a smile in his voice. "Think mouth-to-mouth resuscitation."

Ignoring the heat in her cheeks, she sighed. "I know the mechanics. It's just that—I have a problem."

"Bad breath? Head lice? The heartbreak of psoriasis?"

"Very funny." She tried to make her voice stern,

but couldn't help laughing at him. "None of the above."

"Then what?"

"I've been kissed before and, frankly, I just don't get the point. Considering that, I doubt I can make it look real."

"Well, darlin', whoever kissed you obviously didn't know what he was doing."

Oh Lord, that deep Texas drawl did things to her insides that should be declared a medical emergency. He was smiling, a look that was too masculine and way too cute for her peace of mind.

Suddenly, he stood and crossed the distance between them in two long strides. Looming above her he held out his hand. The fragrance of soap and aftershave and the scent that was uniquely Dev's drifted to her and combined to tie her stomach in knots.

"Help me out here, Hannah. Kiss me, and help me show Ben that it's not enough to make you stay in Destiny."

The sheer masculinity of him stole the breath from her lungs along with her ability to draw in replacement air. Her heart thumped so hard, she was afraid either it would pop out of her chest, or simply wear out and stop so that she needed to shock it into pumping again.

But part of her wanted to know what it would feel like to kiss the guy all the girls had wanted. If the experience was horrible, she could stop wondering about it. But, if as she suspected the sensation was akin to a religious experience, the memory might be worthwhile. On some dark, cold, lonely night, she could pull out the recollection and wrap it warmly around her.

She looked at his large hand, still extended—long, lean fingers, steady palm right there waiting for hers.

Why at that moment did she have to remember that she couldn't remember how many bones there were in the human hand?

"Hannah?"

With a resigned sigh, she placed her shaking fingers in his palm then held her breath as she felt the warm strength when his hand closed around hers. He tugged her to her feet, then drew her to the edge of the circular structure where a slice of silver moonlight chased away the shadows.

"I want him to see us," Dev said, explaining the move out into the open.

"Okay, he spots us. We kiss. Then what?" Hannah wanted to know, her voice annoyingly husky and irritatingly breathless.

"After seeing me kiss you, he'll ask you about it. Guaranteed. Then you can explain to him that our brief encounter of the moonlit kind hasn't in any way, shape or form changed your plans. You can remind him that when your visit is over you're going back to California."

"Okay. Got it."

"Let's put this plan into motion."

Her vocal cords chose that moment to freeze up. All she could do was nod before Dev slid one hand around her waist. He drew her to his tall, solid length. Cupping her cheek with his other hand, he tunneled his fingers into her hair and tilted her head slightly, angling her until he seemed satisfied. Then slowly, he lowered his mouth to hers.

The touch was warm and firm and chaste, yet Hannah half wished they were in a horizontal position. Then all of a sudden her heart started beating faster than it ever had before. An involuntary sigh escaped her and he snuggled her even closer to him. Tipping his head to the side, he made the contact of their lips more firm.

Of their own accord, Hannah's arms found the way around his waist and up his back. Her breasts nestled against the solid wall of his chest as if that's where she belonged. She was soft to his hard, small to his tall, and feminine to his masculine. The sensation brought out all the womanly feelings she'd learned the hard way to suppress.

He traced the seam of her lips with his tongue and without thought or question she opened to him. He caressed the inside of her mouth which became a flashpoint, sending heat radiating through her from the top of her head to the tips of her toes. Excitement cast its spell. There was no room for reason or sanity. She could only feel. Heat, hunger, and heady abandon swept her on a tide of sensual freedom.

Her legs were weak as the kittens she'd watched being born earlier that day. In self-defense, she fisted her hands in the back of his shirt and hung on for dear life. Dev wrapped his other arm around her waist and lifted her off her feet, bringing her mouth to a level with his.

As a doctor she'd found numerous causes for accelerated breathing. But in her experience, never had something so pleasurable set off the condition.

She touched the hair at his nape, finding it silky and soft. With her index finger, she traced the side of his neck, up, down and around to the ridge of his ear. At the barest contact, she heard him suck in his breath and groan. Instantly, his breathing cranked up. How exciting was that! What a heady, powerful feeling, that a man like Dev could be affected by a mere touch from a woman like her.

Finally, he set her feet back on the ground without separating his lips from hers. And how she wished they could stay lip-locked longer, if not forever.

He lifted his head without removing his arms from around her. "That'll show big Ben," he whispered in a husky voice.

"I should hope so," she answered, struggling for just the right tone.

Cooly amused, almost bored was her goal. What she achieved was more like take me, take me now. If there was any justice in that, she was not aware of it.

Dev dropped his arms as if he'd suddenly realized she was a hot rock. He backed up a step and rubbed his palm across the back of his neck. Hannah thought he looked like he didn't know what to say. When was the last time he'd been tongue-tied with a woman? Surely never.

His reaction must have something to do with the fact that he'd actually kissed Hannah Morgan, the brainer misfit who'd tutored him in high school. The girl who hadn't belonged in Destiny ten years ago and still didn't.

Glancing up at Ben's bedroom window, she couldn't tell if he was still spying on them. If the boy had missed out on the show and the intended lesson, she couldn't find it in her heart to care. She'd never in her life been kissed like that. In medical school, she'd had her share of opportunities. But apparently just studying anatomy wasn't a prerequisite for expertise in the field. Dev knew what he was doing. Boy howdy did he ever, she thought still trying to catch her breath. If not for his son, she never would have known that a single kiss truly did pack a powerful punch.

"I think it's high time I went inside," she said, then released a long breath.

"Yeah. I think I'll stay out a little longer while it's cool. A few more weeks and it'll feel like someone stoked Mother Nature's fire."

Hannah felt that way now. But all she said was, "Good night, Dev."

She wasn't staying, her heart warned. But this kiss *almost* made her wish she was.

"Hey, Hannah banana." Ben Hart poked his head in her room, pushing the door a little wider.

"Hey, big Ben."

Here comes the cross-examination, she thought. From her semi-reclining position on her bed, Hannah stared at the little guy and wondered if he knew she'd just called him a London clock. It was early afternoon and she'd been hibernating there most of the day, telling herself it was high time she caught up on her medical journals and periodicals. When she'd been bored enough to open an entertainment magazine, she couldn't lie to herself any longer. Who would have guessed she would be hiding out on Dev Hart's ranch the day after kissing Dev Hart himself?

It was a nice room as hiding places went. It had a queen-size bed covered with a floral quilt in maroon, celery green and white with a coordinating bed skirt. Plush matching shams and throw pillows accented the bedding and she was resting against them now to protect her back from the four-poster, brass bedframe. White wooden shutters held the sun at bay and the walls were a warm beige with white enamel baseboards, raised panel door, and chair rail and crown molding to match. It was nicer than her apartment bedroom in California and this was just the ranch guest room.

But the pleasant surroundings hadn't muted her memory of what she and Dev did in the moonlight. And she had a feeling the moment of truth had arrived. It was time for step two in operation let Ben down gently.

The boy crossed the threshold and sidled up beside her bed. "I saw you kiss my daddy last night."

"You did?"

She pretended surprise, but she was the one jolted when heat flashed through her. The sensual memory was so powerful, it made her glad she was already sitting down.

The boy nodded vigorously. "I saw you in the gazebo last night." He rubbed a knuckle under his nose. "In those movies I told you about, they kissed and lived happy ever after."

"Yeah, I remember that." She was stalling.

"Are you and my daddy gonna get married?"

She would have to teach Ben the finer points of the stalling technique. Darn it all. Dev had been right. Here was Ben asking her about It with a capital I—the kiss. And here was where she'd agreed to remind him that her plans hadn't changed and she was going back where she came from.

She sat up and swung her legs over the side of the bed. "Sweetie, do you remember when your daddy told you that real life isn't like the movies?"

He nodded. "But when you kiss someone it means you love them. Daddy kisses me. Polly kisses me. And I love them."

"There are different kinds of kisses for different kinds of feelings."

"Does that mean Polly doesn't love me?" He frowned and the sparkle in his brown eyes dimmed.

"No." Hannah picked him up and sat him beside her, putting her arm around his shoulders. "I guess what I meant to say is there's different kinds of love. There's the kind I have for my mom and you have for your dad. And the kind of love they feel for you. Then there's the romantic kind, for when you get married."

"And when you have that kind, you kiss in the gazebo?" he asked hopefully.

She shook her head. "Your dad was just giving me a lesson in kissing," she finished lamely.

"You don't know how?" he asked, puzzled.

She did now! "When I was in school, I was really, really smart. Because of that, I finished faster, but I had to work especially hard to do that. I missed out on some stuff and your dad was just showing me."

That sounded good, right?

"You missed out on love?" he asked, wrinkling his nose in confusion.

"No. Well, yes," she admitted.

"So you love my daddy." It wasn't a question.

"I *like* your dad." Wimpy word for what she felt, she didn't have a better one to do her feelings justice.

This was getting her nowhere. If anyone found out she was trying to explain the shadings of love to a four-year-old, they'd revoke her license to practice medicine on the grounds that she hadn't a lick of common sense.

"Ben, was there another reason you stopped in to talk to me?" Please say yes, she silently begged.

His brow furrowed for several moments, then he nodded vigorously. "Daddy wants to see you."

"He does?"

"In his office. Two men came to see him."

"Who are they?" she asked.

"Daddy's friend Mitch and Doc Hol'way. I like him. He gives me a toy when I don't cry."

Hannah wasn't sure whether to be apprehensive that Dev had sent him to find her, or relieved that it was an excuse to terminate this no-win conversation.

She helped him slide down off her bed. "Let's go see your dad."

She followed Ben downstairs where she found Dev in his office, a large room off the foyer. She glanced briefly at the L-shaped desk with computer, white enamel built-in bookcases, and leather wing chairs before she gave her attention to the two men with Dev.

One was a tall, sandy-haired, blue-eyed hunk who would give Dev a run for his money with women. It had been ten years, but she recognized Mitch Rafferty, a championship bull rider and Dev's friend from high school. Now he was the commissioner for the high school rodeo association.

The other was Doc Holloway, a still handsome man in his late forties or early fifties. He was tall, broad-shouldered, and his salt and pepper hair gave him a distinguished air even though he wore jeans and a long-sleeved cotton shirt. His pale blue eyes were intelligent and brimming with humor.

"You remember Doc," Dev said.

"Of course." She couldn't recall a time when he hadn't been Destiny's doctor. He'd taken care of her broken arm.

"Call me Frank," he said. "I'm a good friend of your mother's."

"Nice to see you again," she answered, shaking his

hand. "It's been a long time, but I remember Mitch, too. What are you up to these days besides high school rodeo?"

"I'm involved with a development company. This area is ideal for the next big expansion. The population of Texas is exploding and Destiny is right in the path."

"I'll be sure to duck."

He grinned and the look would melt the average woman into a puddle at his feet. A purely clinical observation since she felt nothing, no heat, weakness in the knees, or accelerated heart rate. Those symptoms only presented themselves when she was with Dev. And she didn't even want to think about what that meant.

"What can I do for you gentlemen?" she asked, careful to look only at the newcomers. She knew if she met Dev's gaze, the memory of his kiss would turn her cheeks to neon pink. She had no desire to explain that to the other two men. "Since I know nothing about urban expansion, I'm going to guess this has something to do with the high school rodeo."

"We need your help, Hannah," Mitch said.

Frank Holloway nodded. "According to the rules, a doctor must be on site in order to hold the championships."

Dev folded his arms over his chest and tucked his fingertips beneath his arms. "Doc was supposed to handle that for us."

"That's right," the doctor agreed. "But I've been called away on a personal matter. My mother is ill and I need to be there," he explained. "I'm not sure how long I'll be gone and I don't want to leave the kids high and dry. Polly mentioned that you were here visiting and suggested that you might be able to help us out.''

''What can I do?'' Hannah asked.

''Be our doctor.'' Mitch met her gaze. ''We're holding the championships on the Circle S, Taylor Stevens's ranch. We'll have a medical station set up and all you have to do is be there. In case of any injuries.''

''Usually nothing happens,'' Doc added. ''Just a precaution. But in an emergency, you might need to stabilize for transport. We'll have a paramedic unit and rescue helicopter for emergencies.''

''What do you say, Hannah?'' Dev asked. ''It's only a week.''

Doc cleared his throat. ''Actually it could be longer than that if Hannah agrees to my proposition.''

''What's that?'' she asked.

''I was wondering if you might consider seeing patients in my office during my absence?'' He stuck his hands in his pockets. ''Your mother has been singing your praises for a long time. I checked you out and she's right. While I'm gone, folks will have to go a long way for medical care, or to the ER, which is a whole lot more costly than an office visit. You'd really be helping me out. Then I wouldn't have to rush back. But take some time to think about it.''

''Okay.'' Hannah didn't need more than a few seconds.

She thought about the magazine upstairs as opposed to a chance to be of use to people. That and the need to take her mind off Dev. Surely idleness was responsible for her preoccupation with him. The frenetic pace of a med student's life was not prone to leisure time. So the explanation made complete sense to her. Instantly her mind was made up.

"Okay," she said again. "I'll do it."

"You're sure about this?" Dev asked. "I know you're here for rest and relaxation."

If she'd needed a booster to convince her, his deep voice raising goose bumps on her arms did the trick. This was a golden opportunity to avoid temptation. Correction—further temptation.

She'd only been there a day and her attraction to Dev Hart was on the verge of an outbreak. She hadn't been enough to make him notice her ten years ago, and certainly nothing good could come of it now. Relationships didn't last. Her mother and father were proof of that. Not to mention Dev and his wife. Along with all the couples she'd seen fall apart in college and medical school. On top of that, her father's desertion had taught her that she was too much trouble to love and she'd been smart enough to take the lesson to heart.

Her attraction to Dev seemed to spread hourly. But anything romantic between them had all the symptoms of cardiac arrest. The diagnosis was clear: Devlin Hart was a walking, talking heartbreak. And she would be wise to take a break from him. This job was just what the doctor ordered.

"I'd be happy to take over for you Doc, I mean Frank." She glanced at Dev. "Rest and relaxation isn't nearly as restful and relaxing as it's cracked up to be."

Chapter Five

"Addie, I'm going to lunch. I've got my beeper and cell phone if you need to reach me."

"Designer doctor from L.A.," the woman mumbled.

Before leaving Destiny, Frank Holloway had briefed Hannah about his practice, his office, and his manager/nurse for the better part of twenty years, Addie Ledbetter. But his briefing hadn't done the woman justice. She was an *I Love Lucy* wanna-be with bright orange hair, big blue eyes, and all the diplomacy of a freshly sharpened scalpel. She could slice and dice without missing a beat. Right now she shook her head, tsked and sighed. Hannah decided that perfectly summed up her own feelings about her first morning filling in for Destiny's doctor.

"I'm a physician, Addie. I live in Los Angeles," she said patiently. "The two are very separate. And what exactly is a designer doc?"

The woman folded her arms beneath her generous bosom. "One with all that frou-frou paraphernalia. A body'd think you were a rocket scientist with all that fancy stuff.''

"You mean Dr. Holloway doesn't use a beeper and a cell phone?"

"When he's not here in Destiny," she allowed. "But Roadkill Café's about the only place in town to eat. It's either that or you brown bag it. Either way I think I can find you without a communication satellite."

Hannah put her hands on her hips. Part of her wanted to laugh, the other part wanted to choke the woman, and to hell with her Hippocratic oath. She wondered if Addie talked to Frank Holloway like that or if it was just her—because she was an outsider.

"I can assure you, Addie, that I'm a good doctor. I like helping people. And I'm serious about what I do. If someone needs me I want to be there."

"If you say so."

Hannah saw no point in trying to convince the woman that she belonged when she didn't believe it herself. During college, med school and all the training that followed, she'd had to prove herself over and over again. Eventually she'd earned grudging respect. But here in Destiny, she'd never fit in.

"I'll be back about one o'clock to complete the charting on the patients I saw this morning."

"That's only thirty minutes."

"I don't need longer than that to grab a bite to eat."

Addie looked at her watch. "Afternoon office hours start at two. I'll be back at one fifty-five."

Hannah nodded. "I'll see you then."

She opened the door and stepped out onto Destiny's main two-lane road. The town had undergone a facelift since she'd lived there. All the buildings had the look of an Old West town, even the computer store on the other side of the street. Doc's office door had an oval, etched glass insert with Frank Holloway, M.D., written in fancy lettering. On the shop next door she saw the name This 'N That, Gifts and Antiques—Maggie Benson, Owner. Hannah remembered Maggie from National Honor Society in high school. She'd always liked the outspoken redhead and thought about renewing the acquaintance. Maybe. Later.

After walking by the hair salon, she stopped in front of the café. Directly across the street was Charlie's Tractor Supply. Standing out front she saw Dev Hart talking to a very attractive woman. So what else was new? In high school he'd always been surrounded by the best-looking girls—except when he'd been learning physics from her. She wasn't even close to being in his league—no matter how much the gazebo kiss in the moonlight might make her wish otherwise. She would always be plain Hannah Morgan and he would be the hunk who attracted women like honey drew a swarm of bees.

The shadow of the wooden overhang shielded her as she stood watching. Mitch Rafferty passed close by, but didn't seem to notice her as he crossed the street. The closer he got to the twosome on the other side, the tenser he looked. He shook hands with Dev, then turned his gaze on the woman who looked familiar to Hannah. Dev glanced across the street and spotted her. The next thing she knew, he touched his hat and said something to his two companions, then walked toward her.

Her heart skidded and she thought about ducking into the alley or the café, but she discarded both ideas. Either course would look like exactly what it was— full retreat.

Dev's boots thunked as he stepped up onto the wooden sidewalk. He took off his black Stetson and ran his fingers through his hair. "Hi, Hannah. How about joining me for lunch?"

He was asking her to sit across a table from him while he turned one hundred percent of his attention on her. It didn't matter that they wouldn't be *completely* alone or that Roadkill Café was far from a romantic spot. The point was that by definition, joining Dev Hart for lunch meant that he would be there. She wasn't prepared to deal with him, no matter how much she might have missed seeing him that morning. One of her reasons for filling in for Doc had been to get away from Dev.

She stuck her hands into the pockets of her navy slacks. "What is this? Take a geek to lunch week?" Inwardly, she winced at her tone. She'd meant it to be teasing, not a cross between shrew and fishwife. "I'm sorry. That didn't come out right at all."

He frowned. "Many a truth…" He shrugged. "But you're not a geek. Why would you think that?"

"Once a geek, always a geek." She tried to smile. "When we were in high school, you never went out of your way to acknowledge me. What other reason could there be for you to do it now?"

He slapped his hat against his muscular thigh. "Ten years ago I was just a kid. How long are you going to punish me for it?"

She tapped her lip. "Indefinitely, I'd say."

What else did she have to use as a shield? Besides, she couldn't seem to stop herself. Being with him alone made her feel like a fish out of water and that feeling did *not* bring out the best in her.

"For cryin' out loud, Hannah, try to look at it from my point of view. I was a guy—"

"'Nuff said," she interjected.

"Male bashing is beneath you," he said, his brown eyes darkening more than she'd thought possible.

"Sorry," she mumbled. "It just sort of pops out."

"As I was saying, in high school I was a guy who could do just about everything well except physics. I wasn't real happy about the fact that I was forced to get help from a girl, a younger one at that."

"You weren't concerned that your jock friends might make fun of you?"

"Of course I was," he agreed. "And you flaunted your IQ like a garlic talisman against a vampire."

"I wasn't that bad," she protested. Was she?

"No? You were pretty darn smart. I was intimidated as hell. But you've changed."

"Do I still need to sneak up on a glass of water?"

He frowned. "That's the second time you used that expression. I have a feeling it's not an accident."

"I overheard you describe me that way to some of your friends. You obviously don't remember."

"I'm sorry, Hannah." He sighed. "But you know as well as I do that there were separate cliques in high school."

"Brainers and jocks," she answered.

He nodded. "And I already admitted that I had some concern about clique-crossover backlash. You can nail me to the wall for this, but frankly you weren't as good-looking then as you are now. You wore glasses practically as big as you were and pardon me for saying this but you were as flat-chested as a boy."

"Thanks for reminding me."

"I wouldn't have said a word if you still were."

She met his gaze and the intensity there heated her skin. "So I'm not that way anymore?"

"Darlin' you've grown up and filled out." He stared at her and his mouth turned up at the corners. "You're fishing for compliments, aren't you?"

"Better late than never," she said.

He ran a hand through his hair. "Look, Hannah, you'd be doing me a favor if you joined me for lunch."

"Really? How?"

"Mitch has a thing for Taylor Stevens."

The memory clicked and she snapped her fingers. "That's who she was. I thought I recognized her. The rodeo championships are going to be held on her ranch."

"That's right. Anyway, he was a little tense when he saw me talking to her and if you join me in the café, it just might take the edge off his temper."

"Be still my heart." She fanned her hand in front of her. It was a flippant gesture, completely useless against the Dev Hart flush heating her skin.

He'd kissed her under the stars until her toes had curled. Now he'd invited her to lunch to keep his friend from being jealous. It suddenly dawned on her that she'd finally gotten him to notice her. Ten years too late and she was less than flattered. Both times the attention had nothing to do with her. But doggone it she couldn't help admiring his honesty. Even she could see that time had improved her looks. But in spite of her efforts not to let it bother her, she felt a twinge of hurt that he'd noticed her on account of someone else.

"So how about it? Will you have lunch with me?"

As much as she wanted to run far and fast, she couldn't say no. "Thanks, Dev. I'd love to join you."

Unfortunately, she found that it was all too true.

He opened the door for her and she preceded him into the café. The interior extended Destiny's Old West motif. A wooden bar, complete with metal foot rail and spittoons, dominated the room. Red-and-white cloth-covered circular tables surrounded by wooden barrel-back chairs were scattered around. The walls sported rodeo photos and various Texas scenes. Beneath them rested booths with plastic pads on wooden benches.

A pretty auburn-haired young woman walked up to them. "Hi, Dev. Hannah."

"How do you know who I am?" she asked.

"You're Polly Morgan's daughter. You look just like your mom."

"Should I know you?" Hannah asked, knowing there was probably a more diplomatic way to phrase it. For the life of her she couldn't think how.

The woman shook her head. "Name's Bonnie Potts. I moved to Destiny after you left."

"I'm so glad. Not that you came after I left," she clarified. "That there's no reason I should remember you. Because I don't. Does that make sense?"

"Perfectly. Table or booth?" she asked, looking from Hannah to Dev.

"Booth," he said.

"Table," she said.

"A booth it is." Bonnie laughed as she turned away and led them to a corner booth nearly hidden by the bar.

Dev's palm tingled when he rested it against Hannah's lower back to guide her across the room. When she moved away from the contact to slide onto the hunter-green leather seat, he found that he missed touching her.

The café hostess pulled out the menus she carried

beneath her arm and handed one to each of them. "What can I get you to drink?"

"Water with lemon," Hannah answered.

"Sweet tea," Dev said.

Bonnie nodded. "I'll give you a few minutes to look over the menu, then I'll be back to take your orders."

Hannah linked her slender fingers together and rested them on the table. "Must be nice," she said.

Her tone was pleasant, but he didn't let that fool him. There was a zinger somewhere in his near future.

"Okay. I'll bite. What must be nice?"

"That women do your bidding. I asked for a table, you said booth. And here we are," she said, holding out her arm to indicate the secluded corner.

"It is nice—when it happens," he admitted, leaning forward as he rested his forearms against the edge of the table. "But that never seems to be when I want it to or for the important things."

"Such as?"

"Getting Ben's mom to stay."

"Oh, Dev—" She reached out, to put her hand on his. A gesture of comfort? Just in time she stopped herself. "I'm sorry. That was uncalled for. I wasn't thinking. I didn't mean to remind you of something painful."

"It's not me I'm concerned about." He didn't hurt anymore, but Ben was another matter. He wouldn't take a chance on a woman unless the relationship was a sure thing. He wouldn't risk his son. "I figure a kid's best chance in this crazy, mixed-up world is to be raised by a mother and father who love him. Ben's not going to have that."

"He's got a father who loves him."

"But his mom left him behind. Someday that's gonna make him different."

"A lot of kids deal with that these days."

"I don't want him to be like a lot of kids. I never meant for him to wonder why he wasn't enough or what he did wrong that made his mom take off the way she did."

"You're going to have to be prepared with answers. Reenforce that it's not about him. It's what she wanted, and her loss."

He met her gaze. "Loss?"

"Ben is a sweetheart and she's missing out on all the precious day-to-day memories. Someday she may want them back. Then it will be too late. But a lot of kids grow up with only one parent and don't do so bad. Me for instance."

"Do you miss your dad?"

"Nope." The shadow that covered her face said otherwise. "And if he walked in that front door right now, I'd go out the back. But that's my choice. And it will be up to the little guy to decide if he wants a relationship with her."

"She doesn't deserve it."

"That will be Ben's decision. And something tells me he doesn't have any trouble making up his own mind."

He laughed. "You got that right." He unrolled his eating utensils from the paper napkin and set them on the table. "He missed you this morning."

"Really?" Her blue eyes sparkled at the words.

He nodded. "He even pretended to be sick so that I'd bring him into Doc's office so he could see you."

"You should have. I would have loved that. He would have been a welcome distraction."

"Busy morning?"

She nodded. "This is the first time I've had a chance to sit all day. I saw everything from male pattern baldness to baby colic."

"The word on the street is that you're the best thing to come to Destiny since satellite TV."

"How do you know?"

He met her gaze. "This is Destiny we're talking about. Small Town, Texas. Any significant news spreads from one end of Main Street to the other by nine-forty-five in the morning."

"Yeah. I'd forgotten that." She frowned.

"What?" he asked.

"The people might be happy with me, but Addie Ledbetter thinks I'm a designer doctor from Los Angeles."

"Give her time."

She plucked at the red-checkered tablecloth. "I won't be here long enough for her to change her mind about me."

"When do you expect to hear on the L.A. jobs?"

"I'm not sure. It could be four to six weeks." She smiled. "Mom is hoping for six."

"So you're going to hang out until you get the word?"

"Unless that's a problem for you."

"Nope."

He liked having her around. Maybe too much. And Ben... He owed Polly. He wouldn't turn her daughter out because his son had a crush on her. Dev would do his best to prepare him for the fact that Hannah wasn't staying. And while he was at it, keep himself from slipping under her spell too. As long as he could do that, he wasn't lying about it not being a problem.

"While I am here, bring Ben into the office any time. He doesn't have to be sick. That little guy has completely stolen my heart."

Right back at you, he wanted to say. His son thought she had wings and a halo—even after he'd seen the two of them in the gazebo and she'd confirmed that it hadn't changed her mind about going back to California.

Boy, that kiss had sure backfired. Ben still had an acute case of puppy love. And Dev couldn't seem to forget the lady doctor and the powerful punch her lips packed. Not to mention her prickly personality.

She was as changeable as Texas weather. The night he'd kissed her in the gazebo, her response had blown him away. He'd never tasted such an intoxicating combination of innocence and passion, sweetness and sin. He hadn't been able to get the encounter out of his mind. Yet today when he'd asked her to lunch, he could have sworn she was deliberately provoking him so he would back off. Why?

He couldn't believe she was still stewing about what had happened in high school. She teased him about women doing his bidding. Was she just the tiniest bit jealous? The thought made him want to grin.

Before he could, Bonnie Potts walked over to the booth, order pad in hand. "Sorry. I would have been back sooner, but I'm doubling as waitress today as well as cook. What can I get for you two?"

"I'll have the burger combo," Dev said without hesitation.

"You didn't even look at that menu, did you?" the woman accused.

"Nobody makes a burger like you," he said with a

smile. Then he met Hannah's gaze. Was there ice in her blue eyes?

"How about for you, Hannah?"

"I'm sorry. I haven't looked yet."

Bonnie grinned. "I'm not surprised. With a guy like Dev sitting across the table, reading a menu wouldn't be my first choice either."

Hannah's gaze flicked to him, then back to the woman. "What do you like on the menu?" she asked.

"It would be easier to tell you what I don't like. And I've got the extra padding on my hips to prove it."

"You're not carrying an extra ounce of fat," Hannah observed.

"Thanks." Bonnie hesitated for a moment. "Oh, hell. I wasn't going to bother you with this, and my timing stinks, but what the heck. It's now or never. Nothing ventured and all that."

"What?" Hannah prompted.

"I'm the President of Destiny's Women's Auxiliary. Once a month we have a luncheon to raise money. To lure the ladies into town, we schedule guest speakers who we hope will be of interest."

"Where does the money go?"

"Into the Sunshine Fund," she explained. "We squirrel away money and let it accumulate until someone in Destiny needs help. Sometimes it's a hard luck story, or maybe just the cash someone could use to plant the seeds of their dream. That's how Maggie Benson came up with part of the capital to start her business."

Dev folded his arms over his chest. "Once the funds went to the high school band members who marched in the Macy's Thanksgiving Day parade in New York.

Another time it was a widow with a baby who needed first and last month's rent on an apartment.''

"What a wonderful idea," Hannah agreed.

"We have a problem this month," Bonnie said, tapping her pencil against her order pad.

"Oh?''

"Doc Holloway was supposed to be our speaker. I thought it might be a good idea to have Doc give us some pointers about taking care of our skin during the hot summer months. The topic is 'Summer sun damage, or how to reduce the signs of aging.'''

Hannah nodded. "That's important all-year round. Especially around here where so many people work outdoors. And with numerous lakes, water sports and pools, people forget about protecting their skin which just happens to be the body's largest organ.''

The other woman nodded. "I'm not sure what we'll do now.''

"Hannah can fill in for the doc," Dev suggested. "She obviously has the smarts.''

Bonnie hesitated. "I really hate to ask. You're supposed to be here for a relaxing vacation and already you're filling in at Doc's office. I wouldn't want to be a bother.''

"It's no bother at all," Hannah said. "I'd be happy to help out. And actually, I have an idea. What about expanding it into a health fair?''

Thoughtfully, Bonnie tapped her finger against her lips. "Tell me more.''

"I could do simple health screenings for high-blood pressure, glucose levels and vision.''

"What if we do some advertising and pull in more folks, I mean other than the women?''

"That would be wonderful," Hannah agreed. "I

could talk to the lab Doc Holloway is using for testing and see if they could do anything for us. The county health department might donate vaccines for kids' immunizations.''

"Wow." Dev was almost dizzy, his head going back and forth between the women. "You two could have planned D Day in half the time."

"Great minds," Hannah said. "Give me the date, Bonnie and I'll put it on my calendar and get to work."

"It's the weekend after the high school rodeo championships. And, thank you," Bonnie said. "That seems so inadequate. I know the other ladies in the auxiliary will be grateful too. And to answer your question, my favorite thing on the menu is the Chinese chicken salad."

"Then that's what I'll have." Hannah handed her menu to the other woman with a smile.

After Bonnie left, Dev noticed Hannah looking at him. "What?"

She met his gaze with a thoughtful one of her own. "Did you get the feeling that I intimidated her?"

"It's not a feeling. You're definitely intimidating."

Her blue eyes widened. "Me? Why?"

"You're smart. You're a hometown girl who made good. You live in L.A. You're sophisticated."

"I'm just plain old Hannah Morgan, the girl who doesn't belong anywhere."

"You don't really believe that."

She nodded. "In high school, I was a brainer geek several years younger than the kids I was in class with. In medical school, friends were hard to make because everyone was older. The professors expected more and gave me grief about looking like a kid. I had to work twice as hard as everyone else to earn a patient's trust.

And now I'm trying to get a position with one of the most prestigious medical practices in the country. I'm smart, and I jumped through all the hoops to get my license. But I know they're still concerned about my age. I'm not complaining, just stating a fact. I don't fit in anywhere." She looked wistfully at the proprietress of the café. "I envy Bonnie."

"Why?"

"Because she's comfortable in her skin, in her town, in her activities."

"Is this because of Addie?" he asked.

"She's just the most recent reminder."

He reached across the table and rested his hand over hers. "Just be yourself, Hannah. If you do that, and put in the time, everything else will fall into place."

"In Destiny?"

He wanted to say "I hope so." Thank God he stopped himself. Seeing Hannah's vulnerability was making it easier for her to get under his skin. He'd always thought she had her act together. She was smart and she knew what she wanted. And she didn't need help from anyone. Now he'd had a glimpse of the scared little girl she'd once been. And maybe still was? He could feel himself being sucked in like debris down the flood control channel. He had to dig in his heels and put a stop to her effect on him.

"You can fit in anywhere you choose. And any pediatric practice in L.A. would be lucky to have you."

He just hoped putting into words the fact that she was going back to California would be enough to get it through his thick skull. Because he couldn't shake the feeling that *he* would be lucky to have her.

Chapter Six

"I don't know how you talked me into this."

Hannah was standing in the corral beside Dev and the two horses he'd saddled. She had agreed to go riding with him and the sight of said horses had made her question her sanity, not to mention commonsense.

"It didn't take a silver-tongued devil," he answered.

"The devil part is true enough," she teased. Then she pointed at him, pretending to be stern. "Don't you say a word about it being as easy as falling off a horse."

"Perish the thought. All I had to do was point out that it's your afternoon off. You had nothing better to do. If you had, I wouldn't have found you aimlessly wandering the house. Be honest. You were bored to tears. It was as easy as being in the right place at the right time with the right words."

"It doesn't make me feel any better that you're right—about all of the above," she grumbled. But she had another reason he hadn't mentioned. Probably because he didn't know. "I don't like the feeling that I can't do something."

And she didn't just mean riding a horse. She couldn't control her feelings for Dev. He *had* found her wandering the house with nothing to do and had suggested a ride. Fleetingly, she'd wondered if he'd been looking for her, but figured that was nothing more than wishful thinking. And how she wished she hadn't entertained that wishful thought in the first place. Because it had made her glow inside and out. And she was absolutely the wrong woman for him.

He wanted a homemaker and she was a doctor.

She was a career woman, a healer who would have nightmare hours because children didn't get sick nine to five. She loved what she did. The best part was the rewards of her hard work would give her mother the life of ease she'd missed out on while Hannah had been growing up. She had a lot to make up to her mom for. And she planned to start as soon as she got the go-ahead on her new job and moved Polly to California.

For now, Hannah stood in the corral with Dev and the two horses. It was time to put up or shut up, she thought.

She glanced at the man beside her. She'd been here on his ranch for three weeks. Except for their single lunch her first day filling in at Doc's office, Ben's birthday party and a short time at dinner each night, their schedules hardly intersected at all. Seeing patients and keeping Doc's practice going in Destiny had kept her running day and night—and sometimes even into the wee hours of the morning. She rarely had an uninterrupted night's sleep. Dev had his hands full with the ranch and preparations to supply the stock for the high school rodeo championships, now just a week away.

All of the above proved they were completely incompatible. Yet her heart had nearly jumped out of her chest at the sight of him. The world's tiniest thought that he might have been looking for her still set her pulse to pounding.

"I'm right about something else, too," he said.

"I know I'm going to be sorry for asking, but what else would that be?" she inquired sweetly.

"It would be a shame to waste that first riding lesson."

"You mean go through a few minutes of fear and terror without any real payoff, in terms of acquiring any sort of expertise?"

"Exactly. And practice makes perfect."

Her thoughts exactly. She needed to practice spending time with him so she could perfect the art of getting her attraction for him under control. And she was well on her way to a cure, if she did say so herself.

Then Hannah saw the grin he flashed and her knees nearly buckled. She put a hand on Trouble's neck to steady herself. Unfortunately, her reaction to him was a glitch in the practice makes perfect philosophy. She was stumbling, mumbling proof that no matter how smart she was, she could still make a fool of herself over a good-looking man.

And there was even more potential to wind up with egg on her face. Because it was way too late to back out of this ride with any dignity intact.

"Has anyone ever told you you're a sadistic man, Dev Hart?"

"It's why all the adoring girls follow me around like I'm the Pied Piper of romance. Just look over your shoulder. They're lurking back there. Thousands of 'em."

She knew the flat Texas landscape, occasionally interrupted by rolling hills, would be hard pressed to hide one woman, let alone hordes. He was making fun of her. And, God help her, she couldn't help being amused. And charmed.

The corners of her mouth turned up. "You're a sarcastic man, too. And this just has to be said—it's not a particularly attractive quality."

He held Trouble's reins in his gloved hand. "I had to cultivate one flaw. We heartthrobs need a protective perimeter. All those women—"

She held up her hand in surrender. "Okay. Maybe I exaggerated."

And maybe she'd missed him. She sighed. There was no maybe about it. This good-natured banter was fun. The fact that he was better looking by far than the average man was a plus. Exhilaration coursed through her and suddenly it was the most beautiful day. The sky was the bluest blue she'd ever seen. The sun was just the right temperature. And all was right with the world. She couldn't be happier that their schedules had intersected.

"Maybe you exaggerated?" One of his eyebrows lifted. "You have some kind of phobia about admitting you're wrong?"

"I don't have a lot of practice. It so rarely happens."

"It's a good thing you're wearing that adjustable baseball hat. If it was a Stetson, the head swelling would cut off the blood flow to your brain. I'm no doctor, but that's got to be bad."

She grinned. "I had to cultivate a flaw, too."

"I can't figure out why you keep bringing the whole women thing up."

"You said it yourself. In a word, heartthrob."

"I was kidding," he protested. "Have you seen me with any women? Besides you and Polly, I mean?"

She thought for a moment. "Actually, yes. I saw you in Destiny with Taylor Stevens."

"That was three weeks ago," he protested.

"You've seen her since then."

He frowned. "I have?"

"There was a picture in the paper—you, Mitch Rafferty and Taylor. In front of her barn. Advertising the rodeo and the upcoming opening of the dude ranch."

He nodded. "Yeah. I forgot about that."

"Selective memory," she muttered. Although she couldn't help being pleased that he'd forgotten.

He handed her the reins then walked around to his horse's left side. "Are you going to pick on me all day or are we going to ride?"

She tapped her index finger against her lips. "Tough decision. Picking on you is tempting—"

"Hannah—" His voice was laced with mock sternness. But the twinkle in his eyes was a dead giveaway that he was teasing.

Something else was in the death throes—like her power to resist him. At this moment, she couldn't find the will to care. Later she would worry about the ground she'd lost. And speaking of losing ground, it was time to get this horseback riding show on the road.

"Okay. I'm finished stalling." Already standing on Trouble's left side, she turned and looked at the worn leather seat of the saddle. She remembered what he'd taught her and muttered, "Everything's left."

Hannah put her foot in the stirrup and leather creaked as she hauled herself a bit awkwardly onto Trouble's back. Dev mounted his own horse in one graceful, fluid, masculine movement that made her mouth go dry. She swallowed once and worked on getting her right foot in the stirrup. The horse shifted beneath her. Recalling what Dev had said about an animal's body language warning a rider, she sucked in a breath and grabbed the saddle horn for security.

"You're okay, Hannah," Dev reassured her. "He's adjusting to the weight of a rider."

"Sure," she agreed. "Makes sense. If someone was sitting on my back, I'd probably notice and have something to say about it."

She could say a few thousand words, including this was only her second—make that third time in the saddle. She'd fallen off the first time. The second, Dev had been behind her. At this moment, she missed the feel of his big body close to hers, the security of his solid strength, his arms around her—protective and strong. But it was all about her fear of sitting on a horse and not about needing him. She wouldn't let herself. He could have any woman he wanted and history had a pesky way of repeating itself. She was still different. It hadn't been right for them ten years ago, and it still wasn't.

As they slowly walked their horses side by side from the corral, she stole a glance at him. He was completely comfortable. Tall in the saddle had never been more three dimensionally clear to her and she couldn't quite stifle a sigh. So much for getting over her attraction. Exposure was causing more acute symptoms. Why?

The answer was simple. And she'd already thought about it. She'd missed seeing him and couldn't resist the chance to spend a little time with him—even in a saddle. Still, she wouldn't be around much longer, so what harm could it do?

They rode in silence for a while, leaving the ranch

buildings behind them. Dev had briefed her, explaining that Trouble was trained to follow his horse and she didn't need to worry about guiding him. She soon realized he was right and with that knowledge, she began to relax.

Hannah stole another glance at Dev, something that rapidly seemed to be turning into a habit. His silhouette and profile couldn't be more masculine. She admired the strong, attractive line of his jaw and lean angles of his cheekbones. He sat straight in the saddle yet easy, one hand loosely holding the reins, the other palm resting on his muscled thigh. The red earth of Texas, dotted with scrub and mesquite, stretched out before them. Snow-white clouds billowed out against the breathtaking blue sky.

"It's so quiet here," she said, with a gusty sigh. "Serene is the word I'd use."

He glanced at her. "I get the feeling it's not a word you get to use very much."

"You're right about that. L.A. isn't exactly the first place that comes to mind when you're looking for peace and tranquility."

"Have you ever thought of moving back here?"

Hannah darted a glance at him and she would have sworn he looked surprised at his own question. "Why would you ask that?"

He shrugged. "I don't know. Stupid question. You've been following your dream almost longer than you lived here in Destiny. And no one knows better than I do that you can't force someone to stay if they don't want to."

"You're talking about your ex-wife."

"Yeah."

Hannah studied his broad shoulders, so wide she believed they could withstand whatever fate dumped on him. He carried the burden alone now, raising his son. She respected him so much for that. He was determined to protect the boy—even from her—because she could never be part of his world. So his question about her moving back was nothing more than making conversation. There was no way it could be more.

"Ben has you, Dev," she said gently. "He's going to be fine. Sometimes we don't get a choice about being raised by two parents."

He slid her a look, shadowed beneath the brim of his black hat. "Is that the voice of experience talking?"

"I already told you—"

"Yeah, practice it somewhere else, Doc. You're angry with your father for leaving."

"What makes you think that?"

"What you said when we had lunch that day in town. One minute you claimed you didn't miss him. The next you said you'd walk out the back door if he came in the front. Call me dull as a widow woman's ax, but my guess is you're sore as hell at him for walking out."

After she got over her surprise that he recalled what she'd said that day, Hannah thought about his comment. "Not mad," she finally said. "Not anymore. I actually think he did me a favor."

"Uh-huh," he said, his tone skeptical.

"Did you ever hear the song about the absentee father who named his son Sue? He knew he wasn't going to be around and wanted the boy to learn how to take care of himself."

"Yeah, I think I did."

"I feel as if my father named me Hank or Rock or Buck. I didn't have a daddy to fight my battles. But I did have a high IQ. You accused me of hiding behind it. I choose to think of it as my best asset. It's gotten me where I am today and I plan to make it continue working for me."

"I think you're blowing smoke, Doc."

"Is that so?"

"There's another song you might have heard. Everybody needs somebody sometime."

"I could remind you of the same thing."

"Touché." He held her gaze for a moment, then turned to look at the trail ahead. "And I need to remind you not to overdo the first time out or your fanny will not thank me." He glanced at her and the heat still lurking in his gaze made her hot all over. "By the way—"

"Y-yes?" How she hated that breathless tone she couldn't control.

He looked at her feet and pointed a gloved finger in that direction. "Tennis shoes are not very practical for riding a horse. You might want to get a pair of western boots."

"Since I'm only going to be here a short time, it seems like a waste of money."

The thought made her sad. Then she got mad. How dare he make her sad that she had to go back to the career she'd worked so hard for? Finally she could see the light at the end of the tunnel. Why did that light feel like it was attached to a speeding locomotive?

She was almost in a position to pay her mother back for being such a burden. When she'd allowed herself to fantasize about this moment, she'd never pictured herself with Dev Hart—or feeling sad.

"You should be hearing about your job interview pretty soon, right?"

She nodded. "Any day now. If not, I'll call."

"I'm glad you're here—for the championships." Leather creaked as he shifted in the saddle. "I mean since Doc Holloway is gone and all."

"I'm happy to be of assistance. Think how bored I'd be otherwise." She smiled at him.

One corner of his mouth curved up as he swayed easily in the saddle. "That reminds me. Mitch said the medical trailer is set up. He suggested you check it out. Doc handled ordering the supplies, but you might want to make sure you have everything you need."

"That's a good idea."

"We can go there now if you'd like."

She shifted in the saddle, her backside starting to feel the effects of the ride. "How far is it? Will my fanny be cursing your name for the next week?"

He grinned. "Just a holler and a half from here."

"Then lead the way," she agreed. "Trouble will surely follow."

Trouble was what she hoped to avoid. Maybe inventorying medical supplies would give her something else to think about besides a captivating cowboy and how he was well on his way to capturing her heart.

A short time later, they were standing in the medical trailer set up behind the portable grandstands trucked in for the championships. Dev watched Hannah ready swabs, gauze and disposable gloves on the tiny counter in the small space. She studied it critically, then rearranged everything.

He didn't think the positioning could be all that important. "You're as jumpy as spit on a hot skillet."

Bent at the waist to peek into the cupboard beneath the counter, she turned her head and met his gaze. "Tell me Dr. Dev, would you care to share with me the symptoms that caused you to come up with that diagnosis?''

"Happy to oblige, ma'am," he said, turning sideways in the trailer's doorway to rest his back against the frame. "You've moved that stuff around five or six times. Now I could be off by a whisker or two, but I'd have to say there's not enough room in here to cuss the cat without gettin' a mouthful of fur. I'd say pretty much everything is at your fingertips. Why are you fretting about where it all goes? You're not worried about this, are you?''

"Of course not." She shook her head, but the shadows in her eyes didn't go away.

"Talk to me, Hannah."

She rested a hand on the countertop. "There's nothing to say. It looks like all the basic supplies are here. I'm just used to the diagnostic equipment provided in a hospital setting. But I can practice kamikaze medicine if I have to.''

"We've got a rescue helicopter standing by if it's necessary to transport someone.''

"I know." She walked four steps to the end of the trailer then turned and came back. The movement of the floor seemed to make her more uptight with each step.

"What is it, Hannah?" He blocked her path as she tried to pass him again. Then he put his hands on her shoulders. Looking into big, bothered, blue eyes, he said, "And please don't insult my intelligence by telling me nothing. Something's got you chute crazy.''

One corner of her mouth curved up. "Chute crazy?''

"Stockman's term. Cattle get nervous about entering a narrow branding or loading chute. Is it the trailer? Do you have claustrophobia?''

She met his gaze for several moments and he thought she was going to ignore his observation. Then she let out a long breath and stepped away, crossing her arms over her chest and curving her fingers around her upper arms.

"It is the trailer, but not because it's small. It just brings back memories." Her gaze flicked into every cluttered corner.

"Bad memories?" he asked gently, encouraging her to talk.

The shadows in her eyes increased as she studied the dreary interior before looking back at him. "The only permanent home I ever had was on wheels—like this. And my mother worked fourteen-hour days to make sure we had that."

"So you *are* angry with your father," he commented.

She shook her head. "No. I'm mad at myself. He left because of me."

"Whoa. You were just a little girl. What could you possibly have done to chase him off?"

She stared at him, her eyes haunted. "Remember when I told you about falling off a horse?"

"Yeah, but I don't see how—"

"I broke my arm."

He took his hat off and ran a hand through his hair. "Well that explains a whole lot. For starters, why riding a horse is bottom of your to-do list."

"It's more than that, Dev. There were doctor visits, medical expenses. The good news is that's when I first thought about becoming a doctor. The bad—it drove my father away."

"Come on, Hannah—"

"It's true. One minute he was there. The next, bills

started rolling in and he was gone. I was too much trouble.''

"Kids aren't a burden. They're a responsibility that comes out of love,'' he said, gentling his tone at the stark vulnerability he saw in her face.

"Not in my case. And I didn't miss him all that much. I was telling you the truth about that,'' she said defensively. She sighed and turned away to fiddle with the box of cotton balls. ''But his leaving put an awfully heavy burden on my mother.''

''It's not your fault, Hannah.''

''I know—''

''Don't blow me off. It doesn't take a master's degree in psychology to figure you out. You blame yourself for what that lowlife creep did. You had an accident and he walked out when you and your mom needed him the most. You were a child. He was the adult who let you down.''

''I understand that.''

''Intellectually, probably. Emotionally—that's a different story.''

''Who died and made you resident shrink?'' she asked, trying to joke.

''I'll be the first to admit that Psychology 101 in college didn't give me impressive credentials. But it doesn't take a mental giant to see what's going on with you.''

''And that would be?''

''You're living in the past. Ten years ago, on top of your astronomical IQ, you felt different because you didn't have a dad. So you isolated yourself.''

''And you think I'm still doing that?''

He noticed that she didn't deny it. ''If the horse

sticks his hoof out, the blacksmith will nail a horseshoe to it.''

''I know you're a rancher, but that one was weird even for you.'' She stared at him for a moment and he could tell she was struggling not to smile. ''What does that mean?''

''Just that it's obvious you're still standing apart—by choice.''

''I can't deny my past shaped me. So did yours,'' she pointed out. ''But every day I'm grateful for where my brains got me. Each experience I've had has made me the strong, capable woman I am today.''

''I don't dispute that—''

She held up her hand. ''Hear me out. I'm on the brink of getting everything I've worked for. As soon as I get that job, I'll have the money I need to give my mother the life she deserves. A house of her own in California—with a permanent foundation on the ground. No wheels. She won't have to work.''

''Your mom might have something to say about that. She's a part of the community and she's got friends here.'' He stopped short of telling her about what he suspected between Polly and Doc Holloway. It wasn't his job to tell her about her mother's love life.

She folded her arms over her chest. ''That might inconvenience you. I'm sorry about that. But my goal is to give her back everything I cost her.''

He struggled to control his irritation. This wasn't about him losing a housekeeper. If Polly wanted to leave, he wouldn't be happy, but he would deal with it. This was about Hannah and the hold those bad memories still had on her.

''That bastard walked out on the two of you,'' he said. ''It's his debt, Hannah, not yours.''

"It is mine," she shot back. "If not for me, he would still be around."

"That's not what a parent's love is all about," he said. "Ask your mother."

"I have."

"And what did she say?"

"That he was too young. That he probably had no intention of settling down with one woman even after saying 'I do.'"

"Polly's smart enough to tell a mule from a race-horse. My guess is that's where you got your brains from."

"She's told me I shouldn't feel guilty."

"Listen to her, Hannah. The problem is his not yours."

"Let's leave him out of the equation. Facts are facts. Mom took care of me, now it's my turn to take care of her."

Dev rubbed the back of his neck. He finally had the whole picture. He completely understood how deep Hannah's pain went and why she held herself back and him at arm's length. Hell, he knew now why she'd been so driven to leave Destiny for a career.

Hannah was a fine doctor. No question about that. The folks who'd seen her in the office for aches, pains, sniffles and stomach upsets would sing her praises from Destiny to the Red River and the Oklahoma prairie beyond. But her dedication to her career swung to the passionate. And now he understood why.

She was determined to make up for driving her father away. His intense frustration at that told him he'd apparently harbored some misguided notion that she would give up her big-city dream and stay. He should know better.

Dev had watched helplessly while the woman he loved raised dust on her way out of town to have a career. Before they married, he hadn't known of Corie's ambition. He'd thought they were riding the same trail as far as life goals were concerned. He'd been wrong. Now he was bewitched by another woman bent on success. It didn't matter that her vocation helped people. Or that she was driven by emotional and unselfish reasons. Or that her goal to pay her mother back would disrupt his life. That was between Polly and Hannah.

His first priority had to be Ben. Then himself if he was to be of any use to his son. Dev knew he would be a fool to give free rein to his budding feelings. An idiot to ride this path when he saw potholes that would swallow him up. Dumb as dirt to let this attraction go unchecked. Burned once, shame on her. Burned twice, shame on him. Now that he knew how deep her commitment went, no way would he let Dr. Hannah Morgan into his heart.

Hell of a thing, finding out M.D. stood for Mega Distraction. Major Dilemma.

My Downfall.

Chapter Seven

On the last night of the championships, Dev waited at the far end of the main corral for intermission to end. The crowd had thinned since there were only three events left: chute dogging, pole bending and bull riding. But since he was a pickup man, he still had a job to do and was waiting for the signal that they were ready to start.

As he stood there, Mitch Rafferty walked by with his arm around Taylor Stevens's waist. Just a few minutes before, in front of God and all the spectators, they had declared what just about everyone in Destiny was making side bets on: they were crazy in love.

Taylor was branching out in a new direction with her dude ranch. Since returning to Destiny, Mitch was working with a development company to bring prosperity to the area. Dev envied them and couldn't help thinking about Hannah. The last time he'd had a Hart to heart talk with her, he'd realized that her childhood memories were not good ones. She'd gone away and made something of herself and was well on her way to a successful life and career in another state. He'd known she was ambitious, but he'd learned how deep it went and why nothing could compel her to stay.

"Penny for 'em."

Dev knew the voice belonged to Grady O'Connor. He glanced to his right where his friend had stopped. "Hey, Sheriff. Penny for what?"

"Your thoughts. You're looking pretty grim. Must be thinking about a woman."

"Remind me not to plan the crime of the century here in Destiny. Considering your sleuthing skills, I wouldn't have a snowball's chance in hell of pulling it off."

"Then let me impress you some more. Would the lady perp happen to be Hannah Morgan?"

"Cuff me and run me in," Dev confirmed.

"What's with you and the pretty doc?"

"Not a blessed thing."

"But not because you're not interested," the lawman guessed.

"Doesn't matter. She's going back to California."

At least now he knew why she was so determined to achieve financial security. For the second time in as many minutes, Dev remembered that day in the medical trailer when she'd told him about breaking her arm and the resulting fallout. He almost smiled at his in-poor-taste play on words. But nothing about the situation was funny.

Grady rested his forearms on the top rail of the fence. "Maybe you could change her mind about leaving."

"Not a chance."

And how pathetic was that? The first woman who'd

interested him in longer than he cared to remember, and she only had eyes for a career. Even if he could let himself compromise his hopes and dreams, Destiny, Texas, would never offer her enough. It didn't do any good to wish things were different. He'd wished as hard as he could that Corie wouldn't walk away from him and Ben. And he'd learned an important lesson. If wishes were horses, beggars would ride.

Grady nudged his hat up with a knuckle. "So you are interested."

"Did I say I was interested?"

"No. But more important is what you didn't say."

"Such as?" Dev demanded.

"You didn't say you *didn't* want to change her mind about leaving, just that there was no chance. It's what you don't say that means the most."

"And you know this how?"

"Because I've known you since high school."

"Then you know I'm not the type to howl at the moon. The lady's leaving. End of story." Dev let out a long breath and stared at the corral where the tractor was smoothing the dirt for the upcoming events.

"For the record, significant others don't grow on trees," Grady pointed out.

Dev slid him a wry look. "That was profound. You missed your calling. Writing a column for one of those lovelorn ladies' magazines would be right up your alley. Not to mention your track record with women would give you the proper credentials."

"I have no track record or credentials," Grady commented equably.

"My point exactly. So who died and put Cupid's bow and arrow in your shoulder holster?"

"Just trying to be a friend."

"I appreciate that. And let me return the favor. I saw you with Jensen Stevens earlier. Is Destiny's small-town rodeo queen turned up-and-coming Dallas family attorney planning to stick around for a while?"

The sheriff's eyes narrowed. "I didn't ask."

"Because you don't care?" Dev wondered how Destiny's finest liked it when the pistol was on the other hip.

"Doesn't matter whether I do or not. It's common knowledge that she'll never get over Zach."

"He's been gone for, what is it now?" Dev thought for a moment. "Seven, eight years?"

"Nine."

"That's a long time to carry a torch for someone," he said. "Sooner or later she'll be ready to move on. Maybe you can give her a nudge in the right direction."

"Even if I was so inclined, which I'm not, I've got bigger fish to fry."

The ragged tone got Dev's attention and he half turned to study his friend. The lines on either side of Grady's nose and mouth seemed to deepen. Tension rolled off him in waves. He'd known Grady O'Connor since high school. The sheriff was rock solid and unflappable. One look at his face said there was something really wrong. For the first time, Dev noticed an envelope sticking out of the sheriff's khaki uniform shirt pocket.

"What's up?" he asked.

"It's no big deal—"

"This is me, Grady. What's going on?"

The sheriff rested his booted foot on the bottom slat of the fence. "I'm being sued."

"What? Why? Some disgruntled perp?"

Grady shook his head. "Custody of the girls."

"You're joking." That shocked Dev more than anything.

"I wish I were."

Grady O'Connor was a good father, good sheriff, good friend. Dev wasn't sure which order he'd put the last two in, but being a father definitely came first with Grady. As far as he knew, there wasn't anyone to challenge his custody of the kids. Grady's family had no cause and wouldn't do that. His wife had passed away and she'd had no other relatives. So who could possibly file a suit with any merit? There had to be something he was missing, or details his friend wasn't sharing.

"Who would sue you for Kasey and Stacy?" Dev asked.

"I'm not sure," the sheriff admitted. "The petitioner is William Robert Adams."

"Related to Zach Adams?"

"More than likely."

"What are you going to do?"

"I'm going to need a lawyer. Jensen offered to help." Grady met his gaze with a shuttered expression. "I turned her down."

"How come? I hear she kicks some pretty impressive legal butt."

"You know why I can't ask her, Dev." The sheriff looked at him again and the intensity in his gaze was unmistakable. "She's the last person who should get involved in this."

"I've got a bad feeling this has something to do with that night at the lake ten years ago."

The muscle in Grady's jaw tensed and released. "I've got the same bad feeling."

Dev nodded grimly. "Is there anything I can do to help?"

"If there is, I'll let you know."

"Just say the word." He thought for a moment. "I saw Jack Riley."

"Me too, with Maggie Benson." Grady grinned fleetingly. "Did you see him jump into the stock pen after Faith fell in? Maggie's daughter sure is a pistol."

Dev smiled. "Yeah. If anyone could use help parenting it's Maggie."

"No kidding. Do you know who Faith's father is?"

"You're the star detective," Dev shot back. "Don't you know?"

"Some things are just beyond my investigative skills."

"I don't think she's ever told anyone. If she had, it would be all over Destiny in thirty minutes."

"It's water over the dam now anyway."

Dev nodded. "I heard Jack was recruited by an elite army force ten years ago, right out of boot camp. Bet he's had some interesting experiences. I'd sure like to hear any stories he has to tell."

"Yeah."

"I've had weird vibes all night," Dev commented. He was remembering that night at the championships ten years before. It was the last time the four of them had been together. "Ever since Mitch showed up… It's as if the past is reaching out and pulling us back."

Grady nodded. "The last time I saw Jack was five years ago. He was here just long enough for his father's funeral, then gone again. Like a covert operation."

"I wonder if he'll stick around a while this time," Dev said. "You could ask him to put all that military training to practical use and take out whoever is behind the lawsuit."

"As an officer of the law, I'm going to forget you said that." Grady smiled, but the warmth didn't reach his ice-blue eyes.

"Okay." Dev thought for a moment. "Still, the weird vibes won't let up. It's been ten years since the four of us were together in Destiny."

"If you use the word 'cosmic,'" Grady said, a warning in his tone, "I'm going to turn my ladies' magazine column over to you."

Dev laughed as he shook his head. "Only if you think the ladies will want an update on the current beef prices."

Grady shook his head. "The four of us back together again. How about that?"

"Yeah. You know, I'm sure Jack and Mitch would want to know if there's anything they can do. About the lawsuit, I mean."

"I'll let you know," Grady agreed. "In the meantime, I'll figure out how I want to handle this. I need to decide how to beat the creep at his own game."

"What creep? What game?" Hannah asked. "You two look deep in conversation. What's going on?" Wearing her white lab coat, she stepped on the bottom slat beside him and looked from Dev to Grady.

"Nothing much," the sheriff said. "The usual. How's it going, Hannah? Saved any lives recently?"

"It's been quiet," she answered. "How about you?"

"I was just about to go keep the peace—or something like that." Grady settled his hat low on his forehead. "See you two later."

"Later," Dev said as his friend walked away and disappeared into the darkness beyond the floodlights.

"He was certainly preoccupied about something," Hannah commented, her head turned as she watched the sheriff until the dark swallowed him.

"He's got good reason to be."

Frowning, she met his gaze. "Why?"

"You'll have to ask him." No way was Dev going to tell her what was going on. It wasn't his secret to share. To distract her, he touched the circular end of the stethoscope looped over her shoulders. "Nice necklace. Fashion statement?"

She caught both ends with her hands and pulled on it. "Habit. I feel almost naked without it."

He'd like to see what she looked like almost naked. The idea heated his blood and sent it racing through his veins, mostly to points south. He needed a distraction. He wished she'd be merciful and do something to take his mind off the sensuous thought. When she didn't, he said the first thing that came to mind.

"You're almost home free," he commented.

"And by that you're implying that the championships are nearly over, meaning I lucked out and haven't had to handle a trauma?" Her words were challenging, but the sting was removed when she smiled.

The beauty of that smile made him feel as if he'd just been tossed off a horse's back and had the wind knocked out of him.

"Yeah, just a couple more events," he managed to answer. "Bull riding is last."

Worry lines marred the smooth skin of her forehead. "That one gives me the willies. There's something not natural about anyone trying to stay on a ton of solid turning, twisting muscle that doesn't want him there."

"It scares the you-know-what out of me, too," he admitted.

"I knew you weren't just another pretty face," she said. "Unlike one of the teenagers I treated yesterday."

"What happened?"

"Up until then, I didn't have to deal with anything more complicated than scrapes, bumps and bruises. But this particular idiot-in-training happens to be a bull rider. His name is Ronnie Slyder and he sliced his hand open on a giant staple."

"Come again?"

"The kids were having squirt-gun fights. He got one of those gigantic ones and the packaging gave him more trouble than an ill-tempered bull."

"Let me see if I've got this straight. All week the kid successfully rides a ton of ticked off bull and he injured himself on a staple?" Dev clarified.

She nodded. "But there's more. After I put six stitches in his palm, he said it could have been worse. I thought he meant that he was lucky he hadn't sliced anything that would impair flexibility in his hand."

"He didn't?"

"Nope. He said if the injury had been to his other hand he would have been really upset."

"Why?"

"That's his rope hand. Since it's okay, he's still planning to ride tonight."

"Is it medically dangerous?"

"*I* wouldn't want to do it," she admitted. "But when he explained how it all works, and I checked with Commissioner Rafferty, I couldn't come up with a medical reason to scrap him. Especially when he said he needs to ride. He's hoping for a college scholarship."

There was an announcement over the public address

system telling the spectators that the last of the events were about to begin.

"That's my cue," Dev said.

"For what? Aren't you a little old to be competing?"

"I'm a pickup man."

"So what else is new?" she asked, a teasing smile making her blue eyes sparkle.

That look turned him inside out and upside down and landed his backside in the dirt. But Dev knew he had to hide his reaction. There was no point in letting her know what she did to him because pretty soon she would be gone and couldn't do it anymore.

"You know, Dr. Morgan, you should come out of your clinic more often."

"It's a trailer, Dev. And why would you say that?"

"Because if you had, you'd know that I'm one of the rodeo's unsung heroes."

"Is that so? Pray tell, why?"

"The pickup man rides—" he held up his hand "—I mean gallops, at great personal peril, into the arena. He pulls the contestant off his irate horse or bull, whichever the case may be, also at great personal peril. Then gets them to safety as fast as possible."

"What we in the medical profession call stat."

"Okay," he said.

"In that case, you are definitely a hero."

Before he could stop himself, he leaned down and touched his mouth to hers. "For luck," he explained. "Gotta git. See you later."

Hannah hung on to the fence as tightly as she was hanging on to her heart. Why had he done that? Ben was home in bed asleep. There was no good reason for him to do that. And now, damn him, her lips tingled.

From the slightest brush of his mouth. A touch that probably didn't mean a thing to him. But, for the life of her, she couldn't work up a really good mad as she watched Dev walk away. How could she get angry at a man who looked that good in denim? Heck, that good from the rear.

Since she knew they could page her to the medical trailer if needed, she stayed to see the final events. It had nothing to do with observing her favorite pickup man, she told herself. Turning her gaze back to the arena, she watched female contestants on horseback swiftly guide their mounts in and out of a line of poles. She marveled at the skill and courage of the riders, groaning when one of the poles was knocked down. She knew that couldn't be good.

The next event was something called chute dogging. It was a lot like the steer wrestling competition except the contestant didn't have to drop from a moving horse. Hannah figured it was probably un-rodeo, un-western, and un-Texan, but she couldn't help rooting for the steer.

Finally, it was time for the bull riding. Mitch Rafferty, rodeo commissioner and former competitor, had told her if the cowboy was bucked off in less than eight seconds, he was disqualified. The point system was more complicated, each contestant's score rising or falling depending on a particular animal and how challenging the ride. She remembered an excited Ronnie Slyder telling her that he'd drawn the most difficult bull for the finals. And he was happy! She didn't understand his youthful excitement at taking a chance. For the first time in her life she felt old. Or maybe just nervous.

Hannah watched when the chute opened and the bull leaped out with the rider on its back, clinging one-handed to a rope loop. After that, she couldn't bear to look. Too hard on her heart. She set her sights on a much more appealing visual—Dev. He was hard on her heart in a much different way.

He galloped into the arena and skillfully maneuvered his horse so that he could grab the rider and rush him to safety. About five or six contestants took their rides, giving her the same number of opportunities to admire Dev's skill and horsemanship. Finally it was time for the very last rider who just happened to be Ronnie Slyder. When the chute opened, she held her breath until he'd stayed on the requisite amount of time. The next thing she knew, he was on the ground and a gasp went up from the crowd. From where she was standing it looked like at least one, maybe more of the animal's hooves had struck him.

The rodeo clowns darted into action, distracting the enraged bull and sending him into the gated enclosure at the end of the arena. Hannah climbed the fence and jumped over, racing to the injured teenager.

"Don't move him," she shouted to everyone who'd gathered around to help. "Get me a stretcher and a neck brace."

She dropped to her knees in the dirt beside the boy. He was on his back, groaning and semiconscious. After checking his pulse, she listened to his strong, steady heartbeat. She moved her hands up and down his arms and legs, inspecting for broken bones. There didn't seem to be any.

"How is he?" Dev was beside her, and worry laced his words.

"As far as I can tell, there's nothing broken. Damn, I wish I had medical equipment. This is like trying to start a fire by rubbing two sticks together."

She palpated his abdomen and there was an involuntary groan from the boy, but he wasn't coherent enough to tell her anything. Just then someone handed her a brace and she immobilized the teenager's neck. Then, along with several other people, she helped lift him onto the back board.

"I want him airlifted to the hospital," she snapped to the paramedics on the scene.

"Chopper's on the way," Dev assured her.

"Good."

The crowd parted and a woman pushed her way through. "I'm Ronnie's mother. How is he, Doctor?"

Hannah looked up into the woman's worried gaze, wishing she had concrete medical facts for reassurance. Wishing she had scrubbed him from the competition. "Pulse and respiration are fine. Heartbeat is steady. As far as I can see nothing's broken, but without tests and diagnostic equipment, that's all I can tell you."

The sound of a chopper overhead filled the air. Within minutes it had landed and emergency medical personnel had secured the teenager on the craft. His mother was allowed to accompany him. And then they were gone.

Hannah looked up at Dev. "This is a hell of a way to end the rodeo."

"Yeah," he said, nudging his hat up.

"I have to go." She turned on her heel and headed for the medical trailer.

"Where? What are you doing, Hannah?" he demanded, falling into step beside her.

"I'm going to the hospital. I need to talk to the doctor there. Ronnie needs a CT scan of the belly to rule out internal bleeding. Probably needs a skull series, too, especially if he hasn't regained consciousness by then.

I want to make sure everything that can be done is. He'll need someone to run interference for him.''

"I'm sure the ER staff is trained to deal with anything.''

"Yeah," she said, looking up at him. "But I was first on the scene. He's my patient. I need to make sure he's okay.''

He let out a long breath. "You have nothing to feel guilty about.''

Her gaze snapped to his. She was surprised he'd known what she was feeling. "I gave him medical clearance even though he only had one good hand.''

"Mitch cleared him too and he used to be a champion bull rider. He would know if an injury to his other hand would be a problem.''

"I'm going to the hospital," she insisted.

"Then I'll drive you.''

"You don't have to—"

"Yeah, I do.''

"It happened in a split second, Dev. There was no time for you to ride in and get him off the bull.''

She recognized surprise when his gaze collided with hers. "Okay. I'll let it go, if you will.'' He rested his hand at the small of her back. "After we go to the hospital and make sure he's going to be all right.''

Hannah intended to argue with him, but didn't have the energy. Some of it had drained out of her from the adrenaline rush of dealing with the emergency. The rest of it she'd used up running from her attraction to Dev. They walked to his truck in silence, giving her time to think.

Since coming back to Destiny, she'd been deliberately hiding behind everything that had happened in high school in order to blunt the force of her fascination for Dev. His ignoring her, saying immature things about her looks. Her pique that he'd finally noticed her, but for the wrong reasons—all of it she'd dredged up and used against him to build a wall to keep him at a distance.

And now here he was driving her to the hospital twenty miles away so she could check on a patient. It was time to admit that Dev Hart was a nice man. She liked him. A lot. But that was the beginning and the end.

She was career; he was cowboy. And never the twain shall meet.

He unlocked his truck and opened the door for her.

"Okay," she said, climbing in. "You can come to the hospital."

Chapter Eight

Dev rubbed a hand across the back of his neck as he sat in the hospital waiting room with Ken and Mary Slyder. He wished he knew something to say that would ease their worry. But if he were in their shoes, and Ben had been choppered in after an accident with a ton of bull, he would be wearing a hole in the floor with his pacing. And that didn't begin to do justice to what he would feel.

Mary sat on one of the room's plastic-covered sofas with her husband beside her, his arm around her shoulders. Overhead, fluorescent lights hummed, giving the room a cold, institutional feel.

The tall, thin brunette twisted her fingers together. "I wish they'd let me go in with him. Why won't they let me see him? That can't be good. I don't think I can stand to wait anymore. What's happening?" she asked helplessly.

"Hannah—Dr. Morgan said she'd find out," Dev reminded her.

"But she's been gone so long. What if they won't tell her anything? She did warn us that she's not on staff here."

The woman's gray-haired husband patted her shoulder. "Don't borrow trouble, honey. If the news was bad we'd know something by now."

"Ken's right," Dev said. "Besides, staff or not, Hannah will find out what's going on with Ronnie. I saw the look in her eyes and I can tell you without a doubt *I* wouldn't want to be the one who tells her no."

He wasn't blowing smoke. Hannah might look like a good, stiff Texas breeze would blow her away. She might be mistaken for a walking blonde joke, until you looked into her big blue eyes. Normally they snapped with spirit and intelligence—and good humor. But when he'd last seen her, they were spitting fire and determination as she'd marched down the hospital corridor on a fact-finding mission. And mission was definitely the right word. Something told him she would have information when she came back.

Hannah Morgan was a hell of a doctor, and a hell of a woman. He couldn't stop himself from wondering what it would be like to have her in his corner. But lickety-split he backed off on that idea. It wasn't safe to go there.

Dev glanced at the double doors and nodded confidently. "Come hell or high water, that woman's gonna get to the bottom of what's happening with Ronnie." He turned his gaze back on the distraught couple huddled on the couch. "Don't you worry. She might not be on staff, but she's a doctor. I have a feeling she won't take no for an answer."

Several moments later, the waiting room's double doors whispered open and the determined doctor in question walked into the room. She was still wearing the white lab coat she'd had on at the rodeo. Her stethoscope was curved around her neck. She wore it like most women wore jewelry. But Hannah wasn't most women. The thought nudged his heart into a canter.

She nodded at Dev, then squared her shoulders and walked to the couple who had shot to their feet at the first sound of the doors opening.

"How is he? What's going on?" Mary Slyder asked. Her husband was right beside her, leaning forward slightly as if he might otherwise miss something. "Is he going to be okay?"

Hannah took a deep breath. "The ER doctor is a trauma specialist. That's a very good thing. Ronnie's in excellent hands with Dr. Elliott. He doesn't think there's any serious damage, but he's ordered a CT scan to rule out internal bleeding. And he wants a skull series—"

"What's that?" Mary Slyder put her fingers over her mouth as the fear in her eyes kicked up a notch.

Hannah reached out and touched her forearm reassuringly. "It's nothing more exotic than X-rays of his head—several different views. It's standard emergency procedure because Ronnie had a contusion and lacerations. And he lost consciousness for a short time. The doctor is concerned about concussion. And he's right to be. I am, too."

The woman brushed away a tear. "How serious is a concussion?"

Hannah let out a long breath. Dev was looking at her face and saw something flicker in her eyes. Somehow he knew she was censoring how much information to give them. She took the woman's arm and led her to the sofa, urging her to sit. With a sigh, Hannah settled on the edge of the plastic beside her.

"If I were you, I'd want the straight story, so I'm going to give it to you."

"Thank you, Doctor," Mary said nodding. "The not knowing is worse."

Hannah nodded. Understanding and comfort seemed to flow from her. "The injury is potentially serious. But there's no reason to panic. The fact that he's conscious now is a good sign." She smiled. "He gave them cause for concern when they asked him what day it was."

"Why?" his mother asked.

"He kept saying it was Friday."

"But it *is* Friday," Mary said.

"They wanted to know the date. But that wasn't the question they asked him." The anxious parents laughed, and then Hannah continued. "Ronnie has a lot going for him. Not the least of which is his hard head."

Dev knew she was thinking that the kid had insisted on riding with stitches in his other hand.

"He can be stubborn," Mary said.

"No bones are broken," Hannah continued. "But until all the tests are in, we only know he's got a bump on his head and a cut over his eyebrow. We know he was lucky that his eye is all right. He's young, tough and in terrific shape—all factors in his favor."

As Hannah talked, listened to questions from the worried parents and patiently answered them, Dev never took his eyes off her. Life and death decisions. He couldn't even imagine what kind of courage it took to do her job. He'd already seen her with Ben and knew she was good with kids. He had no doubt she was a dynamite pediatrician. But he'd never realized that she used completely different skills in handling parents. She was a champ at both.

It had taken years of training and hard work to sharpen those skills for a lucrative practice. How could he ask her to stay in Destiny and give that up? Whoa! Apparently he still hadn't shaken the subconscious hope that she wouldn't go back to California. He was beginning to wonder if he could ever make it go away.

"I want to see Ronnie," Mary said.

"I don't think they'll let you while they're still doing tests." Hannah squeezed the other woman's hand, then looked at the boy's father. "But I'm going back. They're not happy with me, but that's too bad. I plan to continue being a pushy, nosy outsider. I'll keep you informed."

"Thanks, Doc," Ken Slyder answered. "How can we thank you for being here for us—and for Ronnie?"

"Yes," Mary seconded. "It's scary enough. But we appreciate you explaining everything."

"I wouldn't have it any other way," Hannah said, standing. She went to the door. "I'll be back in a little while."

Dev followed her into the hall. "Was all of that the truth?"

"I wouldn't lie to them," she said, sticking her hands in the pockets of her white coat as they walked.

There was a row of vending machines at the end of the hall and Dev put a hand on her arm as she started to round the corner. "Let me buy you a cup of coffee," he offered.

"Thanks. I could use that. Black, please."

He slid a bill into the slot and pushed the button. The cup plopped beneath the spout and the dark, steamy liquid filled it. He opened the clear plastic door and pulled out the container, then handed it to her. As she took it, her fingers brushed against his. The resulting heat was steamier than the coffee.

"So it's looking good for Ronnie?" Dev asked, sticking his fingertips into the pockets of his jeans.

She nodded, then blew on the hot liquid she held cradled in both hands. "There could always be a complication, blood clot, cranial bleeding, internal bleeding. But there was no point in going there with his folks. There's every reason to believe he's going to be fine. Tests are done as much to rule out a problem as find one."

"I know you were frustrated at the rodeo, about not having equipment."

She nodded. "Fortunately in this case, it shouldn't make a difference." She glanced around. "This is a nice facility, the latest equipment and technology. Ronnie is in excellent hands. I'm certain he'll receive the best of care here."

"The Slyders appreciate you being here," he said. "And so do I."

"You? Why?"

Now there was the burning question. He didn't have an emotional connection to the kid other than as a concerned adult, and rodeo volunteer. And a smidgeon of guilt about not getting him off that animal sooner. But somehow, being there with Hannah made everything better, easier. He had a bad feeling it wouldn't matter if they were in a hospital, a five-star restaurant, a corral, or his living room on the ranch. He simply liked spending time with her.

"You're a good doctor, Hannah," he said lamely. He leaned a shoulder against the wall and met her gaze.

"How do you know that? I didn't do anything. How do you know it's not just a job?"

He crossed one boot over his other ankle. "I know you have reasons for wanting to be a success. But it's not just a job. I've seen you in action. You're a dedicated doctor."

She shrugged noncommittally, but there was a hint of a pleased smile on her face. "Anyone can talk to the guy in charge and relay information."

"Yeah, but you could have made a phone call. Not everyone would take the time and trouble to be here at all. You did."

"I'm smart—"

"This isn't about intelligence quotient," he interrupted. "This is about decency and caring. Destiny could use more like you." Dev blinked. He couldn't believe he'd said that.

There it was again, that hint that he wanted her to stay. What the hell was he thinking?

"Thanks, Dev," she answered, then glanced at a spot over his shoulder as if she was afraid he would see something in her eyes. "But all I did was show up. For selfish reasons. I needed to know that Ronnie was getting the best care. If that makes me a good doctor, then I'll accept that."

He noticed she'd ignored his comment about Destiny needing her. But dammit, the town was growing and they could use her skills. He was a concerned citizen. That had to be the reason he'd blurted it out. He wouldn't let it be about wanting Hannah to stick around.

No way did he want to come in a distant second to a woman's career. Not again.

She blew on her coffee. "I have to go be the squeaky wheel and find out everything I can."

He grinned. "Okay. You go, girl. Let me know if you need any muscle."

She nodded, then started to walk away. Her sneaker squeaked on the linoleum floor as she half turned to look at him. "It's late, Dev. You don't have to stay. I'll find a ride back to the ranch."

"I'm the guy who brought you. I'll be seeing you home, ma'am," he said, touching the brim of his hat.

A smile curved the corners of her lips. "Thanks. See you soon."

He watched her walk away, the doctor in denim. He couldn't stop the heat that filled him. The coat hit her at the knee, but he imagined the sway of her hips, and admired her shapely calves and slender ankles. What was it about Hannah that got to him?

Maybe if he'd never kissed her. That night in the moonlight was coming back to bite him in the butt again. So much for using a lesson to his son for selfish purposes. Dev realized *he* was the one who'd learned something.

Tonight he'd seen for himself Hannah's deep-seated enthusiasm and excitement for her work. He should have realized it sooner. She was a passionate woman. From firsthand—or should he say mouth-to-mouth experience—he'd found that out. He'd bet the farm that she was capable of deep personal feelings. The man she cared about would be a lucky son of a gun.

"But it won't be me," he said to the row of vending machines. "I can't take the chance."

Hannah was too keyed up to go into the house. "I think I'll stay out here for a little while," she said to

Dev as they walked past the gazebo on the way to the front porch.

He had driven her back to the ranch after the results of Ronnie's tests had all come back negative. The cut above his eye had required three stitches, which he said would impress the girls. The doctor was keeping him in the hospital overnight to be on the safe side. And all was right with the world, she thought with a happy sigh.

"I'll keep you company." Dev's voice was deep.

The husky quality made her think of tangled bodies and twisted sheets.

"That's not necessary," she protested. "It's been a long day and you get up before God."

"Someone has to tell Him to start the world," he said.

Hannah noticed something else about his tone. In fact, all the way home from the hospital he'd hardly said two words.

"What's wrong, Dev?"

He sat down on the wooden steps leading up to the porch. Hannah settled beside him, knowing it probably wasn't the smartest move she'd ever made. The sparks she felt from just the barest brush of their shoulders confirmed her suspicion.

"Does it show?"

She was surprised he didn't blow her off. "Yeah. Want to talk about it? Does it have anything to do with Ronnie Slyder getting hurt?"

"Indirectly, I guess." He rested his forearms on his thighs and let his hands dangle between his widespread knees. "I kept picturing Ben in that hospital."

"Yeah," she said. "Me, too."

Hoping the move looked casual, she slid away from

him, putting a couple of inches between herself and the heat of his body. If only it were as easy to shut out the masculine scent that was so Dev.

"I'd like to wrap my son in plastic and keep him safe," he admitted.

"Be sure there are airholes in the protective covering. It's hard to breathe through plastic," she said, trying to lighten his mood.

"I'm serious, Hannah. Kids think they're immortal."

"Personally, I think anyone who would voluntarily get on the back of a ton of bull needs a psych evaluation."

That flippant remark actually rewarded her with a small smile. Then he stared into the darkness again. "I'm not just talking about the rodeo. Although I'd like to lock him in a room, or hire a twenty-four-hour-a-day bodyguard, I know Ben needs to be allowed to grow." He ran a hand through his hair. "I'm talking about decisions kids make that can affect the rest of their lives. How do I teach him to do the right thing? How can I be sure he'll do what's best for him and the kids he's with?"

"This is more than Ronnie, isn't it?"

He met her gaze for several moments, then nodded. "I talked to Grady tonight at the rodeo."

"I saw you. He left just as I arrived. Is something wrong?"

"He's got some legal stuff going on."

Hannah tucked a strand of hair behind her ear then linked her fingers and rested her joined hands in her lap. "Since he's the sheriff, that's not a stretch. He's sworn to uphold the law, I'd say that's in his job description."

Dev shook his head. "It's personal stuff and it's trouble."

"What?" She looked at him for explanation. It was like staring at a sphinx. "Yanking out a hot appendix isn't this hard."

"Something happened, Hannah. Ten years ago."

"What?" she asked again.

He shook his head. "I— Hindsight is twenty/twenty. I could have done something. Things might be different if only I'd—" He stopped and rubbed a hand across the back of his neck. "I wish I'd had my head on straight back then. I was just a kid. We all were. But it's done now."

Standing, he took several steps, just to where the glow from the porch light butted up against the shadows. He folded his arms over his chest and stood staring into the darkness.

Hannah wanted to stay where she was, after all she had a front row seat to admire his spectacular cowboy butt from a safe distance. But she couldn't. With a sigh she pushed to her feet and walked the several steps to where he stood. She only hesitated a moment before resting a hand on his upper arm. The muscle flexed beneath her fingers and she resisted the urge to wrap both hands around the masculine curve.

"I can't say anymore than that," he said.

"Okay. But I have something to say, and you're not going to like it."

He looked down, then covered her hand with his large, warm palm. "Unless you're going to offer me an inoculation against teenage trouble, I'm not sure I want to hear it."

"You have no idea how much I wish I could." She sighed. "My job would be so much easier. I deal with the highs and lows all the time. As far as Ben is concerned, all you can do is your best. Sometimes all you can do is nothing. When he was learning to walk, you had to stand back and watch him fall. Sometimes it hurt—you more than him. But if you'd picked him up and carried him, granted you would have saved him pain at the time, but he wouldn't be running now. When he started to talk, if you'd anticipated his needs before he could voice them, there would have been no reason for him to say the words.''

"There are times I wish he didn't," he said with a grin.

"You don't really mean that," she chided gently.

"No. And I know you're right. It's just that looking back at my adolescence, if only I'd—"

"Don't," she said, taking her hand from beneath his and settling it on top of his fingers. She squeezed lightly, willing him to absorb her words. "It's tempting to second-guess yourself. It's so easy when the pressure's off to look back and critique. To see what you could have done differently, maybe better. With kids, we let go, watch them wobble, stretch their muscles, walk, run, grow and mature. No pain, no gain. Maturity is the great equalizer—or something like that." She rested her cheek against his arm for a moment and sighed. "Sorry. I seem to be spouting clichés like an uncapped oil well."

"No big deal."

She lifted her head and looked up at him. "You're absolutely right. Hindsight *is* twenty/twenty. If we could see into the future we would probably all make different decisions, on the spot."

"Not everything," he said.

His voice had that husky quality again. It raised

goose bumps on her arms. Because she was still touching him, she felt the exact moment when he tensed. His gaze found hers and his eyes turned smoky and intense.

"What do you mean?" she asked breathlessly.

"I could never regret this."

He turned the hand she was holding and captured hers, pulling it to his chest. As if they were about to start the steps of a difficult dance, he placed his palm over her fingers, trapping them against the strong, steady throb of his heart. She got the feeling he was listening to a tune that she couldn't hear as his other arm encircled her waist, drawing her slowly to him. Warmth from his skin seeped through his cotton shirt to the sensitive nerve endings in her fingertips. Heat from his hand burned through the material of her blouse and branded his touch into her back.

Her breasts pressed against the solid, unyielding wall of his chest. Hannah knew she was brighter than the average bear and had been all her life. But right now, she didn't have to be the brightest star in the sky to know that Dev Hart intended to kiss her.

She froze as he lowered his head. It would be stupid to let him. It would be dumb to ignore the fact it was all about the attraction sizzling between them and not because he cared deeply for her. It would be idiotic to forget that attraction and forever-after were as far apart as Texas and California. But for the first time in her life she wanted to forget, ignore, overlook and disregard her superior brain, and wallow in hormone heaven. She actually *wanted* to be a dumb, stupid idiot.

As his lips touched hers, she found that this foolish state worked for her, more than she'd ever thought possible. His mouth was firm yet soft, taking and giving, seeking and sampling. Liquid heat flowed through her veins and pooled in her belly, radiating outward. She didn't need a dermatologist to tell her that her skin was flushed and hot. Or a pulmonologist to diagnose her shortness of breath. The cause was at once simple and complicated.

Dev.

He shifted slightly, then removed his hand from hers. The light evening breeze caressed her exposed knuckles even as his palm closed over her breast. The longed-for contact made her forget to breathe as she seemed to swell into his hand. Her skin tingled through the material of her bra and shirt. She felt like the princess and the pea, sensation in spite of all the barriers. Against all the odds.

Just like she and Dev were a long shot.

What were the odds that she would wind up kissing one of Destiny's most eligible bachelors a second time? Until this magic moment, she would have guessed slim to none.

It was time to stop thinking and just feel. Let go. Her nipple puckered at the same time she arched her back, urging her breast more securely into his palm. She heard his quick intake of breath at her response, and felt his other hand tighten at her waist.

He traced the outline of her lips with his tongue, and instantly her mouth opened, admitting him inside. She heard the harsh rasp of his breathing and took supreme satisfaction in her feminine powers. But satisfaction of a different sort stole over her as he stroked the roof of her mouth, sending desire arcing through her.

He lightly kissed the corner of her mouth and nibbled his way over her cheek and jaw. Her breath caught as he slowed to a spot in the sensitive hollow just behind her mandibular joint and below her earlobe. She was sure she would die of sheer pleasure when he caught it between his teeth and tenderly tortured her. But that was nothing compared to the pure and simple sensual exhilaration she felt when he stroked the oh-so-responsive spot with the tip of his tongue.

She squirmed in his arms, pressed herself even closer to his warmth and solid strength. Her hand stole up his chest to his neck where her fingers channeled into the hair at his nape.

"Oh, Dev," she whispered. "That feels so wonderful."

"Hannah, I— Damn." He let out a frustrated breath.

The next thing Hannah knew, he wasn't touching her anymore. He'd stepped away. She opened her eyes and blinked, trying to stifle her disappointment.

"I can't do this," he said.

She didn't know what to say. Define this? Make love to her? Take her now? All of the above? Nothing? Then she got what *this* was. He didn't want her. She couldn't believe she'd been so foolish. She'd wondered what it would be like to finally have Dev Hart notice her. Now she knew. It would be humiliation and mortification.

It was just like ten years ago. He didn't want to go any further with her. Didn't want to know anymore about her.

"I can't do this either. It's late. I have to go in." She ran trembling fingers through her hair, then turned away.

"Hannah, wait—"

"What?" she asked without looking at him.

He cursed under his breath, then huffed out a sound of frustration. "Nothing. You're right. It's late."

She walked up the steps and into the house without

looking back. It was late, all right. Too late to take back what she'd just done. But tomorrow was another day.

It would bring her closer to the time when she would leave Destiny. And Dev.

If only that thought brought her comfort instead of profound sadness and wrenching pain.

Chapter Nine

At noon, Dev walked toward the house. He was tired, hungry and cantankerous. The last Newy had pointed out and Dev had been forced to admit, if only to himself, that his foreman was right. Although, Hannah was to blame—for the tired and cantankerous part. Oh, he'd started it, just about eleven hours ago. But she'd kissed him back. Romantically rusty he might be, but his instincts couldn't be that wrong.

If only she hadn't looked so beautiful in the moonlight, he might have been able to resist her. Maybe if she hadn't smiled her sweet, innocent Hannah smile. The warmth had made her glow brighter than the sky's most brilliant star. And he didn't even want to think about how good she had smelled. Or how soft she'd felt in his arms. The way she tasted—

Damn. He couldn't *stop* thinking about her.

He entered the house through the service porch, leaving his hat on a hook there. On the way to the kitchen, he stopped in the washroom to clean his hands and face. He wished rinsing away memories of kissing Hannah were as easy as getting rid of the grime he'd picked up during morning chores. After drying his hands and face, he walked into the kitchen and found Polly setting the table for lunch.

She glanced at him over her shoulder and smiled. "Hi, Dev. I hope sandwiches are okay."

He nodded. "I'm so hungry I could eat a bear."

"You wouldn't be if you'd eaten a decent breakfast," she pointed out.

"Wasn't very hungry then." He took a glass from the cupboard above the sink and filled it with water, then drank. "What're you up to this afternoon?"

"Since you're riding with your child, I decided to spend some time with mine," she said brightly. "She's been so busy filling in at Frank's office, we've hardly had any time together."

It was Saturday and Hannah didn't have to see patients today. That meant she would be around. He'd wanted to stay as far away from the house and nearby outbuildings as he could get, but he'd promised Ben he would supervise him on his new horse.

"Sounds fair," he said. The idea of spending time with Hannah not only sounded fair, it was more appealing than he wanted to admit. But the fact was, he'd like to hang out with her, too. Every day, that feeling got bigger and harder to ignore.

Kissing her hadn't been the stupidest thing he'd ever done. But probably in the top five. As much as he wanted to block out the memory of just about the best kiss he'd ever had, even more he wanted to erase the last look he'd seen on her face. Hurt and humiliation. He knew she was thinking he hadn't wanted her.

The truth was he'd wanted her more than his next breath.

And he'd thought seriously about sweeping her into his arms and taking her upstairs to his room where he could have loved her all night long. Her artless, eager response to his kiss told him she probably wouldn't have objected. But there was a problem. Actually, off the top of his head, he could think of more than a dozen, but there was no point in going there.

In the nick of time, he'd realized that a single night with Hannah wouldn't ease his longing. He had a feeling that loving her, tasting her in the most intimate way a man could know a woman, would only make him want her more. That thought was about as welcome as a skunk at a lawn party.

He'd wanted to explain and take away her pain, but he'd stopped himself. It was smarter just to break it off, maybe cancel out the dumb move.

Before he could worry the idea anymore, the doctor of his dreams walked into the room.

"Hi, honey," Polly said. "Did you make your call?"

"Hi," she said, her cheeks turning a becoming pink when she glanced in his direction.

She was wearing a hot pink T-shirt and white shorts that revealed shapely legs he instantly pictured wrapped around his waist. So much for not working himself up into a lather.

"Hi," she said to him.

Dev folded his arms over his chest. "Afternoon."

When their gazes locked, he winced at the expression in her eyes. It was as if someone had pulled the plug on the light. That someone was him. She wrongly thought he didn't want her. If only he could tell her how much that wasn't true. But if he did, it would open the door back up for him to do something she would rightly hate him for. The expression "between a rock and a hard place" had never been more true.

"What call was that?" he asked, just to make conversation, he told himself.

"Actually I made two," she said. It was the cool, aloof professional doctor's voice from last night at the hospital. "I checked on Ronnie Slyder."

Polly set a pitcher of sweet tea on the table. "Hannah told me what happened," she explained to Dev. "How is the boy, honey?"

"He was discharged this morning with orders to see his family doctor next week."

"What was the other call?" he asked.

Polly tucked a strand of blond hair behind her ear, then gave him a teasing look. "Who hit you with the nosy stick?"

"Just being friendly," he explained.

Only partly true. He found he wanted to know everything about Hannah. What she did when she wasn't with him. What she was thinking and feeling. What she was doing for the rest of her life.

"I called to check on my first choice job in California," she answered. "I've received two offers, but neither is the one I've been hoping for."

To hell with the nosy stick. He felt as if he'd just been hit by a truck on the information highway. His reaction was crystal clear proof that she'd just told him more than he should want to know—especially about the rest of her life. If he had a lick of sense, he would leave it at that. Unfortunately, now that he'd eased out into traffic on the info highway, he kind of needed to go with the flow. When you made conversation, you'd best be prepared to keep talking whether or not you liked the answers you got.

"California?" he prompted. "This is Saturday. Was anyone on the job there to give you an answer?" He held his breath against the pain.

"The office manager works half a day." She folded her arms over her chest and leaned a hip against one of the ladderback chairs surrounding the table. "One of the advantages of a medical group is enough people to expand office hours and take calls without overloading anyone. Medicine is a service-oriented profession. Medical professionals need to be available twenty-four hours a day."

Polly put a plate of lunch meat and cheese in the center of the table. "Don't keep me in suspense, Honey, what did the office manager say?"

She sighed. "No word yet. They have a final interview, some hotshot one of the doctors is high on. After that, all the partners are going to meet and make a decision. Probably a week to ten days more." She met his gaze. "I hope it won't be an inconvenience for me to stay a little longer."

Did her chin go up slightly, just a shade defensively? As if she were protecting herself in case he was of a mind to throw her out? Nothing could be further from the truth. If anything he wanted to ask her to stay permanently, give up the job in California. If they didn't appreciate her enough to make her their number-one candidate, it was their loss.

If she stuck around, it would give them a chance to see what this attraction was between them. But, she'd made it clear her career path didn't lead to Destiny. Hannah felt the need to give her mother what she believed in her heart she'd cost her. Considering that, she wasn't likely to look kindly on any suggestion about giving up a profitable practice in the big city to come back home. And after what had happened with his wife, he would be an idiot to ask. If he did, he would need first aid, or better yet, a fire extinguisher. He was this close to getting burned twice.

"You're welcome to stay as long as you need to," he said.

"Thanks. I appreciate it."

He met Hannah's gaze. "So what are you ladies planning to do this afternoon?"

She rubbed the chair back with her thumb. "I need to go into town to work out some details for the health fair next weekend."

"Then we're going shopping," Polly said. "A new outlet mall opened up not too far away. I want to take Hannah."

"Can I go with you, Polly?" Ben wandered into the room just in time to hear the last part. "Hi, Hannah banana."

"Hey, big Ben," she said, smiling at him with genuine warmth.

Dev felt like he was on the outside looking in—cold. Living outside the fire, too far away to get burned, yet feeling the absence of beneficial warmth. The only heat he felt was hot under the collar. Since when would Ben rather go shopping than riding?

But he knew the answer. Since Hannah. He wasn't jealous; he was worried. In spite of his efforts, the boy was getting attached to her.

"Hey, son. I thought you wanted to ride your horse this afternoon."

"You don't really want to go shopping," Polly said, putting a basket of rolls and bread on the table.

"Do too." The boy thrust out his lower lip. "I want to go with Hannah."

She bent down to his level and took his hand. "But you've been waiting for your dad to watch you ride your new horse."

"I can do that any old time. But you're not gonna be here much longer." A sparkle stole into his brown eyes as he slid his chubby little arm around her neck. "But maybe—"

"What?" Hannah prompted.

"I saw you kiss my daddy last night. Does that mean you're gonna stay?"

"Really?" Polly looked from her daughter to Dev.

Well that woke up the Indians, he thought. As if he needed another complication for his son's feelings. He forced himself to look sternly at the boy. "You should have been asleep. And to answer your question, Hannah hasn't changed her mind. She just told me she'll hear about her job in California real soon now."

"I hope they fire you," Ben said, puffing out his lip again.

Hannah laughed. "They would have to hire me before they can do that, big guy." She looked at Dev, then her glance skittered away. "But I can promise you one thing, you won't see me kiss your dad again."

"If you do kiss 'im, does that mean you'll stay?" the boy asked, clearly not giving up.

Dev sighed as he reminded himself that determination would be a positive characteristic in a man.

"No," Dev said. "Hannah's not staying and it's time you got that through your head."

He knew he sounded harsh and hated it. But he didn't believe in encouraging false hope. There would be no third time's the charm, and no happy ending.

Dev couldn't take a chance on Hannah. He was a grown-up and deserved the consequences of his own stupidity. But he wasn't the only one getting attached to her. And Ben was just a kid. He wouldn't put his son in a position to be hurt again.

The health fair was almost over but Hannah wouldn't breathe a sigh of relief until it was. She'd kicked off the event with her talk on skin cancer prevention at the Women's Auxiliary luncheon. Her message: sunscreen and more sunscreen. And she figured she could use a bucket of it about now. Even though her long table was set up in the shade under the overhang outside Doc Holloway's office, it was hot and the sun kept shifting.

She'd been in demand since one o'clock when the luncheon was over and people had begun to wander over to the health fair. Sheriff O'Connor had roped off Main Street where Addie had helped her set up stations for specific medical screenings.

Her office nurse had trained Bonnie Potts on the machine to do blood pressure, pulse and temperature readings. The nurse was doing vision screenings which left Hannah with finger sticks and the glucometer for blood sugar readings.

She fixed a bandage on Ginger Applewhite's finger. The thirty-something woman was married to the owner of Charlie's Tractor Supply and clerked in the store.

"So do I have to give up Twinkies, Doc?" the tall brunette asked.

Hannah frowned. "Yeah, it's on the high side, Ginger. I'd like to send you to the lab for a fasting blood sample. Why don't you call Addie for an appointment so we can talk about it and set things up?"

The woman nodded. "Should I be worried? Am I gonna keel over between now and then?"

"This is only a screening. And it could just be that snowcone I saw you eating."

"It hit the spot, as hot as it is," Ginger said.

"That's why I want to get a fasting sample." Hannah handed her one of Doc Holloway's business cards with the office phone number. "It's important to rule out anything serious."

"Okay. I'll call on Monday." She smiled. "Thanks Dr. Morgan."

When Ginger walked away, an older man stepped in front of Hannah. "I can check your blood sugar," Hannah offered.

"Nope. I'd rather paint my barn pink," the man said. He was tall, in his early sixties, lean and white-haired with piercing blue eyes. "Addie says to give these to the doc." He held up a piece of paper that had the results of his screenings.

"I'm Dr. Hannah Morgan," she answered.

"The hell you say? Why, you're just a baby."

"Potty-trained just last week," Hannah muttered under breath.

"Nothin' wrong with my ears," he said.

"I'm glad to hear it." Hannah thought her face would crack from the smile she plastered on it. The name on the paper he'd handed her said Clovis Evans. "Nice to meet you, Mr. Evans. I'll just take a look at your work-up sheet."

"Nothin' wrong with me," he answered.

"You look like you're in excellent health." Hannah scanned the numbers on the paper, then frowned. "I see here that your blood pressure is high. I'd like you to go back to where Bonnie Potts is and have her repeat the reading.''

"She already did that. Told me to tell you second time said the same as the first.'' Worry dueled with defiance in his expression. "What's wrong?''

Trying to decide how to handle the situation and how much information to give him, Hannah frowned at the sheet. She didn't want to frighten him needlessly. At the same time, she needed to impress upon him not to disregard the screening. She met his gaze. "Mr. Evans, high blood pressure can be a serious condition.''

"How so?''

"It's often referred to as the silent killer because it can result in a stroke or heart attack without warning.''

"I feel fine,'' he insisted, and stubborn was written all over his face.

She nodded. "That's part of the problem. If you felt like something the cat dragged in, you'd do something about it. But it's hard to believe anything's wrong when there are no symptoms.''

"What do I do?'' he asked, rubbing a hand over the back of his neck.

"I'd like to see you in the office. We need to discuss the possibility of medication to control your blood pressure. Also diet and exercise can help.''

"Look, little lady, it's not like I sit around the ranch all day and do nothing.''

"I'm sure you don't. And there's no need to worry prematurely—''

"Who says I'm worried?'' he snapped. "I'm healthy as a horse.''

"Ignoring this condition could lead to a problem

that's as bad as you're thinking. I'd like you to call for an appointment—''

''Maybe when Doc Holloway gets back—''

She straightened to her full height and still had to look up at him. ''Mr. Evans, have you ever heard the expression that when you bury your head in the sand, you leave your fanny exposed?'' Hannah asked.

''Look, missy—''

''Clovis, don't start.'' Addie Ledbetter walked over and put her hand on one substantial hip, then stared hard at the man. ''I don't want to see you giving Doc Morgan a hard time.''

Hannah couldn't believe her eyes and ears. The woman who had exhibited every single symptom of perpetual PMS had actually come to her rescue like the marines to an unarmed third-world country. Certainly Addie's attitude had softened in the weeks since Hannah had been filling in for Doc Holloway. But defending her to one of Destiny's senior citizens was like waving the white flag. She'd turned her away from the dark side and Hannah wanted to kiss her.

Clovis Evans cleared his throat and shifted his weight from one boot to the other. ''Now Addie, you got no call to get mad as a hen in a wool basket.'' He darted a skeptical look in Hannah's direction. ''She doesn't look more'n eighteen years old. And she's a woman to boot. Why should I listen to what she's tellin' me?''

Because I spent hours and hours studying, Hannah wanted to say. Because I worked my tail off and learned and I know what I'm talking about.

''*I'm* a woman,'' Addie pointed out. ''I'd be careful about that sort of thing if I were you, Clovis Evans. Now as for the doc, she went to school for a lot of years and she's sharper than a pocket full of toothpicks. I've seen her in action and she knows what she's doing.'' The plump redhead pointed at the crotchety man. "You listen to her, mister, because I'm telling you to. We'll see you bright and early Monday morning.''

"Okay, Addie. If you say so.'' Sheepishly, he looked at Hannah. "Thanks, Doc.''

"You're welcome,'' she said. Meeting the other woman's gaze she asked, "Well what do you know?''

"I know you're doing a good thing,'' Addie said. "Clovis Evans will thank you and so will his family. This health fair is a fine idea, a real service to the community.''

"I wish I could take credit for it, but they're happening everywhere. When you calculate time and money, it's an inexpensive way to screen for medical problems. And a real service to a community.''

"A big-city idea?'' Addie asked with a sly smile.

Hannah grinned back. "I'm not going there. It's just a great opportunity to reach out in a nonthreatening way.''

The nurse surveyed the stragglers still meandering around the stations. "If we'd had more time to get the word out, we'd have had a lot more people to nonthreaten.''

Hannah laughed ruefully. "If we'd had more people, I'd have needed a whole lot more help and equipment.''

"Next year we can plan for that,'' the other woman said.

"I can write up some notes for Doc Holloway in case there is a next year. But I won't be here.''

Hannah felt a tug in the general region of her heart at the words. With profound regret, it hit her that she really was leaving Destiny. It had been a good day. She'd won over Addie Ledbetter. She had reached out to the townspeople and they had reached back. She was beginning to make friends. They had listened to her. At least most of them. Addie the enforcer had brought Clovis Evans around. But between the health fair, the trauma at the rodeo and seeing Doc's patients for the last few weeks, she hadn't felt so much satisfaction in her job for a long time. Was it because she'd had an opportunity to become more personally involved? Because it was a small town where everyone knew everyone else? What would it be like to practice medicine in Destiny?

With a large sigh, Addie sat down beside her and slid a stack of papers over in her direction. "Next year is three hundred and sixty-five days away. Plans have a way of changing," she said wisely.

"Not these plans."

"What plans are those?"

That was a question Hannah wouldn't ordinarily have considered answering. But then she saw the sympathetic look in the other woman's piercing blue eyes. The words came pouring out before she could stop them.

"I'm waiting to hear on a job in California. I'm going to make a lot of money and give my mom the easy life she deserves."

"So Polly's moving to la-la land?"

"That's the plan."

"Hmm."

"What does that mean?" Hannah asked, frowning.

Large shoulders and plump arms lifted in a shrug. "Your mom might have something to say about that.

She and Frank Holloway could just have different ideas.''

Hannah stared at the other woman. Her mother had never hinted at anything between herself and Doc. Before she could say more, a familiar freckle-faced four-year-old showed up in front of her. And just two steps behind was the familiar father. She found it extremely disconcerting the way her heart kicked up at the sight of the man.

"Hi, Hannah banana."

"Hi, yourself."

"I have to go," Addie said. "Got company coming for dinner tonight."

"I couldn't have done this without you. Thanks for everything, Addie. See you Monday."

"Count on it, Doc."

When the redhead smiled and winked at her, Hannah was completely shocked and embarrassed at her own reaction. She wanted to cry. Fortunately with a certain cowboy and his adorable son standing in front of her she managed to pull herself together with some discreet blinking.

"What's going on?" she asked, looking from Dev to Ben.

"I got my eyes checked," the little boy announced proudly.

Hannah glanced to the empty station, where the vision chart was still displayed with the big E at the top. How she'd hated that as a girl. Without glasses and eventually contacts, she hadn't been able to see much below that letter.

"And how are your pretty peepers?" she asked the child. Surely he was fine. From his bedroom window, little eagle eyes had quite clearly seen her kiss his father in the gazebo and again by the front porch.

"Boys don't have pretty eyes," he scoffed. "And anyway, Addie says mine aren't so good," he finished glumly.

"Really?" she asked, her gaze shifting to Dev's.

Sometimes with children so young the screening was difficult because they didn't know the alphabet. "Did you know all the letters?"

"Yeah, he did," his father confirmed.

Dumb question. Ben showed all the signs of being very precocious, and if anyone should know it was her. She'd skipped the grades in school and had the emotional scars to prove it. Her only excuse for forgetting was Dev's close proximity. Her brain seemed to go into suspended animation whenever he was around. If this had happened so acutely ten years ago, her tutoring wouldn't have helped him get through elementary math, let alone physics.

"Here's his results," Dev said, handing her the sheet.

"Hmm," she said, imitating Addie.

It was such an all encompassing word. Was it a word? Maybe not. But it sounded good and bought her some time. The results showed that there was some difference in his eyes. The right was twenty/twenty which probably enabled him to compensate for the weakness in his left eye. His slightly less than perfect vision hadn't hampered his ability to see Dev kiss her. The memory caused her heart to flutter and her pulse to skip. Her temperature shot up and her BP would probably rival Clovis Evans's.

"Daddy, can I go see Polly?"

Dev glanced to the spot where Hannah's mother was

standing talking to Bonnie Potts in front of the Roadkill Café. "Sure, son. I'll be there in a minute."

Hannah studied him as he watched his son scamper over to her mother. In his expression worry, pride and love wove together in equal parts.

"This is just a screening, Dev."

"Yeah."

"Before he starts school, it's good to know if there's anything going on with his eyes."

"Okay."

"I suggest taking him to an ophthalmologist for a more thorough exam, preferably one who specializes in children," she suggested.

"I'll do that." But his forehead was still creased with worry.

"Are you concerned about his vision, Dev?"

"I worry about everything." He met her gaze and something in his brown eyes told her he didn't just mean the child's physical well-being.

She recalled a week before when the boy had said he'd seen them kissing. Dev had agreed with her that it wouldn't happen again. Was he just not interested in her enough to bother? Or had he been protecting his son?

"I'll be gone soon," she said. Was she trying to reassure him or herself that her departure would solve their problems? "That'll be one less thing for you to worry about," she said, trying to snap him out of it with humor. Unfortunately she found nothing amusing in leaving Destiny.

"I heard you tell Addie that you won't be around next year. But the look on your face said you wanted something different."

Was he reading her so right on because he *wanted*

her to stay? Or had she really betrayed her feelings? That surprised her almost as much as the fact that he'd been able to figure her out so easily. She *had* been torn about leaving and wondering what it would be like to stay in Destiny.

"You saw all that in one look on this face?" she said, crossing her eyes. "No way."

"I like that face." There was a husky, seductive note in his deep voice.

Along with a hint of yearning? He was the reason she'd even momentarily entertained the idea of staying in Destiny.

He was also the reason she had to leave before it was too late.

Chapter Ten

Just after ten at night, Dev walked into his dimly lighted kitchen. After returning to the ranch from the health fair, he'd learned his prize mare was about to foal. She had a history of difficult births and he wanted to be there. Ben had insisted on going with him but had soon lost interest in the long process and had gone back to the house to see Hannah.

He couldn't blame the boy for that. The same inclination was something Dev fought on an annoyingly regular basis. Maybe that was why he felt tired to the bone, he thought, standing at the sink while he finished washing his hands.

"Hi."

Even with the noise of the water running, one small word was enough for him to know her voice. It was a seductive tone, smooth and soft, with just a dash of whiskey and warmth thrown in to make it interesting. So very like her. After shutting off the faucet, he turned to study Hannah standing in the doorway, a book in her hand, wire-rimmed glasses perched on her nose.

"Hi." He grabbed the towel from the holder on the cupboard, then leaned against the sink as he dried his hands.

"Are you handing out cigars?" she asked. "Did the horse have her baby?"

He nodded. "A boy. Mother and son are doing well."

"I'm glad."

Without a speck of makeup, barefoot and wearing an oversize T-shirt and cutoff sweats, she looked good enough to pull into his arms. Which he couldn't do. If he touched her he'd be a goner. She was temptation with a capital T.

"Anyone else awake?" he asked.

She shook her head. "Mom turned in early."

"I know it's late, but what about Ben?" He prayed he wouldn't be alone with her.

She smiled fondly. "He made it until all of eight-thirty. After protesting that he never gets tired, he was asleep in about thirty seconds. I guess the health fair wore him out."

"You were a big hit in town."

"Not me. But I think the event went pretty well."

"You *are* the event. Without a doctor it would never have come off."

With one slender ankle crossed over the other, she rested a shoulder against the doorway frame and pressed the hardback book to her chest. "I did enjoy getting to know the people in town better."

"I think the feeling was mutual."

Dev remembered telling her that she isolated herself behind her astronomical IQ and the circumstances of her father's abandonment. But that's not what he saw today. She joked, talked and laughed with everyone from infants to the elderly. Addie Ledbetter had been riding shotgun, but Hannah had still convinced stubborn Clovis Evans to agree to an office visit. He was happy about her triumph today. But something was bothering him and he couldn't put his finger on exactly what.

"Destiny's mutual admiration society?" She shook her head thoughtfully. "Maybe with everyone but Clovis Evans. It's my expert medical opinion that the man needs a personality transplant. At the same time, I believe I could surgically remove his excess cynicism," she said.

He laughed. "I won't tell you the man's not difficult. But he's the salt of the earth."

Suddenly she straightened and snapped her fingers. "Speaking of salt, Mom said to tell you she left a plate of food in the refrigerator for you."

"I can't decide whether I'm more hungry or tired," he admitted.

She walked over to the table and pulled out a chair. "Then sit yourself down, sir. I'll warm up your dinner."

"You don't have to. I can do it. I wasn't hinting or anything."

"Sure you were." She opened the refrigerator door and glanced at him over her shoulder. "Besides, I know I don't have to. I want to. It's the least I can do to say thanks for all your hospitality."

The beginning of goodbye.

Dev was too tired to fight the regret he felt at the thought that she would be gone in a week. The idea of this big house without Hannah in it made him bluer than the panhandle sky. And that could explain what was bothering him about seeing her interact with the people in town today. She fit Destiny, just like the right size glove. If she hadn't, would it be easier for him to say goodbye?

"Do you know when Doc's coming back?" he asked.

"I talked to him just before the health fair. He said he would be back day after tomorrow. His mother is doing fine now and he knows I'm leaving in less than a week."

"It's been nice having you here, Hannah."

Nice? Who was he kidding? Nice didn't come close to what he was feeling. She'd put a shine on his life. He always looked forward to coming home to Ben after a long day's work. But it was more than that with Hannah. He felt an excitement, a spring in his step, an urgency just to see her that he'd never experienced before. Not even with Corie.

"And I've enjoyed spending time here." She took the foil covering from the plate, leaving only plastic wrap on the food. "You're going to love this—roast, mashed potatoes, gravy, okra. Mom did the homecooking part. But I would be happy to take all the credit for warming it to perfection in the microwave."

He couldn't help grinning and that surprised him. It had taken most of his energy to trudge from the barn to the house and he'd have sworn he didn't have enough left over to smile. Hannah had put the lie to that.

He sat down at the table where a place setting waited for him and let his gaze devour her, storing up sustenance—memories of the smartest, prettiest thing this side of the Rio Grande. "You're a shameless glory hog, Doctor."

"Nobody's perfect."

When the microwave beeped, she pulled the plate out and set it on his placemat. Steam wafted above the food as she lifted off the covering. Her glasses fogged up and he reached over to take them off since her hands were full wrestling with the condensation-coated plastic.

"My hero."

"Happy to oblige, ma'am."

"I took out the contacts. My eyes were tired." Smiling sheepishly, she took them from him and wiped the lenses on the hem of her T-shirt.

"I hear that." He'd *felt* that too. An indefinable something, a sizzle of awareness that always happened when his fingers brushed Hannah's.

He'd bet a dollar to a doughnut that he wasn't the only one. The sudden color in her cheeks and shy flutter of her lashes, the way her gaze skittered away from his, not to mention how quickly she pulled back—all of that added up to the fact that she'd noticed the intimacy. He wanted to encircle her waist with his arm and pull her closer to him, settle her on his lap. Instead, he picked up the fork by his plate and scooped up a bite of mashed potatoes and gravy.

"Would you like a beer?" she asked.

"Yeah. Thanks."

Her bare feet slapped against the tile floor as she padded back to the refrigerator. He followed her movement and decided the view from the back was equally as good as the front. Her shirt was baggy over her shorts—until she bent over. Then the material molded to her curvy backside, beckoning him. Damned if his palms didn't start itching. Funny how a pretty, sexy lady could chase the tired right out of a man.

Not just any woman. Hannah.

She tried to unscrew the cap of the beer. Taking the hem of her shirt, she put it around the top of the bottle and attempted to twist it off. "I need a man," she said, bringing it to him.

"Happy to oblige, ma'am." He easily removed the cap and took a long swallow, trying to ignore her innocent intimation.

"I loosened it for you," she said, avoiding the minefield where he could easily be persuaded to go.

He looked up at her beside him. "You really hate when you can't do something, don't you?"

"I much prefer to be in control at all times," she admitted.

"Wouldn't we all. But as a pediatrician, you should know as well as I do that kids are a reality check as far as having the upper hand."

"That's true—"

"Daddy?"

Dev turned. As if on cue, he saw Ben standing in the doorway. "Hi, son."

Sleepily rubbing his eyes, the boy stumbled across the room. Dev scooped him up when he got close enough, then set him on his thigh. "What are you doing up?"

"Not sleepy."

"All evidence to the contrary," he said, meeting Hannah's amused gaze.

"Huh?" the boy said, then yawned.

"Never mind. Did you have a bad dream?"

"Maybe." Ben nodded. "And I wanted to kiss you good night. Did Lizzie have her baby?"

"A boy," he said.

"Can I name him in the morning?"

"Sure. Everything okay?" Dev asked.

The child nodded and snuggled trustingly against him. "Now you're here."

The words warmed Dev clear through and he looked at Hannah's face. There was such longing in her expression. Somehow he knew she was wishing her own father had been around. She would never admit it because it was something she couldn't control. She'd claim it was over and had made her strong and resilient. But it made him want to throttle the man who'd abandoned her. The jerk didn't deserve the label father. He wondered if that experience was another layer in her determination to leave. If she was afraid to trust him. Beware of men because they walk out?

He dragged his gaze from her pretty face and studied his son's sleepy expression. "Are you ready to go back to bed?"

"I think I'm tired now," he answered with another big yawn.

Beside him, Hannah moved slightly, enough to stir the air. Dev could smell her fragrance. It was a combination of soap and the unique scent of her soft skin.

"Hey, big Ben," she soothed. "How about if I take you back up to bed while your dad eats his dinner?"

"Are you hungry, Daddy?"

Dev glanced at her mouth. "You have no idea, son."

"Then it's okay if Hannah tucks me in."

Thank goodness the boy was too young to notice the dazzling, sensual currents running between himself and Hannah. If he did, the inevitable questions would be tough to answer.

"Thanks, pal." He hugged the boy close for a moment, then kissed the downy hair on top of his head. "'Night, big Ben," he said. "I love you."

"Love you too, Daddy."

When he was alone, Dev thought about how he'd started using the nickname Hannah had given his son. He wondered what else would remind him of her after she was gone. What else would torture him when she wasn't here at night? But he knew the black hole in his life after she left would be torment enough.

A few minutes later she returned and her presence filled up the empty spot in the kitchen. Dev met her gaze when she sat at a right angle to him at the table. He set his fork on his empty plate, then pushed it away. He took the last swallow of his beer, hoping it would dull the need for her that was building inside him.

"Did you slip my son a sedative?" he asked to fill the silence.

"Of course not," she scoffed. "Why?"

"He's not notoriously easy to bed down. I figured it would take you so long, I wouldn't see you again tonight."

And he realized that would have bothered him more than a little.

She shrugged. "It wasn't much of a challenge. I read him a quick story, turned on his night-light, and kissed the little procrastinator good-night."

If she kissed *him,* Dev thought, neither of them would go to sleep. At least not any time soon. The thought made him hot all over and he blew out a long breath. He had to stop this foolishness. That's all there was to it.

Otherwise he'd be thinking he was in love with her.

And that just couldn't happen. He didn't trust the emotion. He'd given in to it once and failed. This time, he didn't have only himself to think about. And Hannah had three strikes against her: she lived fifteen hundred miles away, she was a career woman and she wasn't likely to look kindly on a guy who'd made fun of her ten years ago.

The devil of it was that Ben seemed to have fallen for her, too. If her world record time tucking him in was anything to go by, she seemed to have a positive effect on both of the Hart men.

He couldn't help wishing he'd had the good sense to notice her in high school. Would they have a chance now if life hadn't butted in and turned him into a cynic? Unfortunately, experience had made him a cautious man who was just this side of bitter.

"Penny for your thoughts?" Hannah said.

Funny, he recalled the sheriff using the same expression. He'd never considered himself the reflective sort, but maybe that was something else he had Hannah to thank for.

"Trust me. They're not worth that much," he answered.

"I doubt it."

His gaze lingered on her mouth. How he wanted to taste her softness again, drink of her sweetness and fire. But they'd agreed no more kisses. What would she think if he trashed their bargain? He swore she was already on his wavelength when her eyes widened slightly and her breathing quickened.

He leaned closer to her. "Hannah, I—"

Suddenly the phone rang. In the quiet of late night it startled him. Since Hannah had been at Doc's, it happened on a regular basis. Dev knew he should be used to it by now, but he wasn't. Hannah didn't blink an eye.

"I'll get it," she said, jumping up to lift the receiver on the wall phone by the hall doorway. "Hello?"

She'd moved so fast, he couldn't help thinking she was glad that something had interrupted them. As he watched, her expectant, dreamy look disappeared, replaced by an intense expression. He recognized it—from the rodeo when Ronnie had been hurt, and at the health fair he'd seen her go into doctor mode when she'd told Clovis Evans about his high blood pressure. She was wearing her professional face now.

"When?" she asked. Nodding, she said, "Tell them I'll meet them at the ER." She hung up and turned to him. "That was the answering service. I have to go, as soon as I change my clothes. A sick baby."

"Do you want me to drive you?"

"No. You're exhausted and you've got to get up at dawn and tell the Lord to start the world. I'll be fine. But thanks," she said.

Then she was gone.

A few minutes later, Dev heard the front door close.

The good news was the sick baby was in good hands. The bad: he was getting a preview of life without Hannah just a little sooner than he'd wanted.

But that was good. Wasn't it? He needed a kick in the behind to remind him that she was a good doctor married to her job. Unfortunately, the man who let himself love her would have to share her with folks who needed her skills. That foolish man would be abandoned like this on a regular basis.

Dev was glad he'd been smart enough not to let his own feelings get out of hand.

"I'm going to hell for that lie," he said, feeling the loneliness like he never had before.

* * *

"It's nice to have you back, Frank." Polly Morgan smiled at their dinner guest as she set a tossed salad on the table.

Hannah met Dev's gaze as she put the cloth-lined basket of rolls in front of him. There was a gleam in his eyes and she knew he was going to say something, but couldn't imagine what was going on behind that handsome face of his.

"It is good to have you back, Doc. Hannah's been burning the candle at both ends lately."

Was he sticking up for her? Hannah wondered. No one ever stuck up for her. It was too sweet for words, though completely unnecessary. She'd just been doing what she'd trained so hard to do. But now Doc was back. He'd returned to work in Destiny that day and Hannah had invited him to dinner—at her mother's instructions. When she looked at Polly's shining face, Hannah knew at least one of the Morgan women was happy to see him. For her, it meant one step closer to leaving. The thought made her stomach fall like the blood pressure of a patient bleeding out.

But, she reminded herself, tonight she had some good news to share. And she tried not to spoil it by thinking about how going away was going to tear her apart.

Dev and Ben were already sitting at the table along with their guest while Hannah helped her mother set out fried chicken, potato salad and rolls. Finally everything was ready and Polly sat down beside the doctor.

Hannah took her place at a right angle to Dev. "*I'm* not ashamed to admit that I'm glad you're back too, Doc. I don't know how you handle the practice alone. I haven't worked that hard since I was an intern."

Ben squirmed with excitement. "Doc, Hannah fixed that baby."

"He makes me sound like a cross between Mac the mechanic and Madame Curie," Hannah said.

"If the shoe fits," Doc said, his eyes twinkling.

"The baby just needed meds for fever, an IV and time to kick that nasty virus she got from her big brother. She's home now and doing just fine."

Hannah wished she could say the same for herself. With two measly days left in Destiny, she had to be the walking, talking picture of gloom. And her mother was the exact opposite. The woman glowed like a smitten schoolgirl. Hannah wasn't exactly sure how she felt about that.

Ever since Doc had arrived a short while before, Hannah made it a point to observe the two of them together. She hadn't been able to forget what Addie had implied, that her mother and the widower doctor were an item. But she couldn't see anything special. Addie must have been mistaken. Or did Hannah just not want to see it?

She watched them talk and still couldn't detect a single clue that they shared more than friendship. Polly was just excited at the prospect of a dinner guest.

The clink of dishes and the murmur of voices filled the air as food was passed around the table. When Hannah wasn't keeping an eye on her mother, she stole peeks at Dev. It felt like storing up memories, small puzzle pieces for one large heart-stopping picture for when she wouldn't be able to see him.

"So, Hannah," Doc said, interrupting her thoughts. "Things at the office were okay while I was away?"

"Fine," she answered.

"You didn't have trouble with Addie?" he asked, a knowing look in his eyes.

"You mean like when she accused me of being a designer doctor from Los Angeles?"

He laughed. "Yeah, like that."

"It took a while," Hannah admitted. "But I think I won her over."

Dev forked up a bite of potato salad. "At the health fair, she and Addie tag-teamed poor Clovis Evans. They played good cop/bad cop. Three guesses who was the bad cop and the first two don't count."

"I'm not saying I'd want Addie involved in diplomatic relations," Doc said. "But she keeps my office and everything in it, including me, running like a well-fed quarter horse. She's a good nurse and underneath that abrasive exterior is a heart of gold." He chewed thoughtfully, then added, "Everyone in Destiny is still talking about the health fair. You throw a great party, Doctor."

Hannah felt herself flush with pride at his words. "It went well. But I didn't do it by myself. A lot of people helped."

Polly smiled at the doctor, then beamed in Hannah's direction. "She's just being modest."

"Doc, Hannah 'zamined my eyes," Ben chimed in.

"Not exactly, big guy," she said. "I just interpreted the data."

"Huh?" the boy said, looking at her as if she had two heads.

"Hannah just means she did a good job, buddy," Doc said laughing. "Something tells me it will become an annual event in Destiny. Although if it grows as much as I think it will, I'm not sure I can pull it off alone."

Hannah met his gaze and felt an air of expectation. The sparkle in his eyes made her think he was leading up to something. "What?" she asked.

Doc looked at her mother in a way that Hannah could only think of as intimate. When Polly smiled at him and nodded slightly, it had all the characteristics of couple's shorthand, a wordless form of communication between two people who were close.

Doc cleared his throat. "Hannah, I'd like to offer you a partnership in my medical practice," he said.

"Hannah doesn't hafta practice. She already knows how t'be a good doctor," Ben said.

"No, son. Doc offered Hannah a job," Dev explained to the boy.

"Does that mean Hannah's gonna stay here with me?"

"I don't know," Dev said, looking at her. "Does it?"

His tone gave nothing away. But the intensity on his face sent her heart into premature atrial contractions. Translation: a nonthreatening accelerated heartbeat that meant she was so not over wanting him. His brown eyes were filled with such yearning that she wanted to reach out and put her arms around him. Because she couldn't, her heart ached with something that a nitro-glycerin tablet wouldn't help.

Doc put down his fork. "Say something, Hannah. I think we'd make an ideal team—I'm an internist and you're a pediatrician. Not to mention that a lot of my female patients would love to have a woman to talk to. Your mother says you haven't heard yet about the number-one job opportunity in California. So what do you say?"

She sat motionless for a moment, staring at the man

who had just complicated her well-thought-out career plan. Then she looked at Dev Hart, the man who had made a career out of complicating her well-thought-out personal life.

"Wow. My mother was a bit premature about that California offer. So many jobs, so little time," she said. "Not to mention that the commute would be a killer."

"What are you talking about, Hannah?" Polly asked, her forehead puckering with confusion.

"I got the call today. They came through with the job I've been waiting for."

Ben was bouncing in his chair. "So you're stayin' here, right, Hannah banana?"

"Did you take the offer?" Dev asked.

Her gaze was drawn back to his as if he were a lighthouse in a storm. "Yes." She looked across the table at Ben. "I have to go back to California, big Ben."

Brown eyes just like his father's filled with tears. "No." He shook his head. "I don't want you to. Stay here," he begged.

"I can't. Sweetie, please listen—"

"No." He slid off his chair. "I don't like you anymore." Tears began trickling down his cheeks just before he ran out of the room.

She put down her napkin and she started to stand. "I'll talk to him."

"No." Dev put his hand on her arm.

The yearning she'd seen moments before on his face was gone, replaced by anger. A muscle in his lean cheek contracted and his mouth thinned to a straight line. Then he got up and followed his son from the room. Did Dev hate her too? Every part of her cried out against it. She couldn't stand the thought that he hated her because—

Oh, God. She loved him.

Why now was it so clear to her? When she'd devastated his child and he'd looked at her as if he wished she would disappear, why did she realize she'd probably been in love with him since she was sixteen years old?

Some doctor she was. All the telltale symptoms were clearly exhibited. Racing pulse whenever he was near. Accelerated heart rate at the merest sight of him. Weakness in the knees when he smiled that bone-melting smile.

And if all of that wasn't enough proof, there had been something else that should have convinced her. When she'd been offered her dream job, she'd felt like she'd just been condemned to life in prison without the possibility of parole.

For a split second, she wondered maybe. Maybe she could stay. Maybe she could take Doc's offer and not leave Destiny. She was finally learning to fit in and folks seemed to accept her. Then there was Dev. And Ben. Father and son had both stolen her heart. All they needed was time. Right? Would it be smart—?

Smart. Her only asset. How could she have forgotten? When her father had walked out, she'd learned she would never have a mother *and* a father. In all the time since, nothing had happened to undo the lesson that she should never expect to have it all. She could have the job she wanted—but it was in California. She could fall in love—but the man lived half a country away in Texas. She could finally fit in somewhere—but she would have to leave.

But she'd forgotten the first, best lesson—Don't be stupid.

Falling in love with Dev had been stupid. But she didn't have to compound the fracture to her heart. She didn't have to stay. She was in a position to have everything.

So much for being smart. She'd learned that everything didn't include Dev Hart's love.

Chapter Eleven

"**Y**ou look like someone just cut the ears off your favorite stethoscope." Polly slid her a sympathetic look.

"They're not ears, Mom," Hannah said.

She was standing at the sink, rinsing the dishes her mother was washing by hand. Dev and Ben hadn't returned to the table. It had been over an hour and she hadn't seen them since the child had said he didn't like her anymore and the father had given her the hate stare.

"I feel like something Dev would scrape off his boot in the barn," Hannah admitted.

"I'm sorry, sweetheart. Try not to fret about it." Polly scrubbed the pan in the sink.

"I can't help it. I'm a pediatrician, for goodness' sake. Did you see Ben's little face? I took an oath to heal the sick. What kind of person am I?" she wailed.

"Ben doesn't understand. He'll get over it."

"He's a bright boy," Hannah argued. "But all he understands is that I'm leaving him."

"And he's right," her mother pointed out.

"It's not about him."

"Then it's about the money?"

"Yes. No." Hannah rested her hands on the edge of the sink and leaned forward shaking her head. "It's not that simple."

"Let me ask you something," her mother said. "When Frank offered you a partnership in his practice, did you give it serious consideration?"

"Of course, I did."

Polly gave her the this-is-your-mother look. "Don't forget I was there. It took you all of thirty seconds to turn him down."

"I've worked hard for that job in California. And I'd already accepted it when Doc made his offer."

"California is a job—not a partnership," her mother pointed out.

"It will lead to one. Things are different in Los Angeles." Hannah took the frying pan from her mother and rinsed it, then set it on the drainboard. "The starting salary and profit sharing will give me what I need," she defended.

"And how much do you need?"

"Enough to buy you a house. Enough so you don't have to work ever again. Enough to make up to you for everything you lost on account of me."

Polly stopped washing a large bowl and stared at her. "Is that what this is all about? Paying me back?"

"It's more than that. My father walked out because taking care of me was too much trouble. On that day, you started working two jobs—three when you add mothering me into the equation." Hannah toyed with the frayed edge of the dishrag. "You were always working to put food on the table, a roof over our heads and clothes on our backs. By my tally, I figure I cost you a life.''

''Since when is love about keeping a tally?''

''I didn't mean it like that—''

''Yes, you did.'' With her wet hands hanging over the sink, Polly half turned to face her. ''Let's get something straight. Your father was an immature, skirt-chasing wanderer who never intended to put down roots when he married me. I told you this already and I thought you understood.''

''I did—''

Her mother shook her head. ''Apparently you didn't. Let me say it again. You fell off that horse and broke your arm because he was too busy hitting on a woman to watch his own daughter. He left because he didn't love *me* and never could. It had nothing to do with you.''

''You never told me he was hitting on someone.''

''He's your father.'' Polly let out a long sigh. ''I didn't want to completely trash the man to you. But now it seems I've done you a disservice by not giving you all the facts. And it's not just him. We were young, Hannah. I got pregnant with you. I suppose I was lucky he agreed to get married. At least I avoided an ugly label for you. But that's all I'll give the jerk.''

''The fact remains that you sacrificed a lot for me.''

''Oh, sweetheart.'' Polly took her hands in her own soapy wet ones, apparently unaware that she was dripping on the floor. ''It was never a sacrifice. It's not an obligation when you're a mother. You're the best thing that ever happened to me. I would do it all over again—under the same circumstances. I took care of you the best way I knew how. I love you.''

"I appreciate that, Mom. I love you, too. And that's why I want to buy you a house and give you things."

"I don't understand."

Hannah squeezed her mother's hands. "I'd like to move you to California. I can take care of you for a change. And we can do things together, make up for lost time."

"We can't ever get that time back. We just need to make every moment we spend together a special memory." Polly shook her head. "Not only that, I like my life here just fine."

"But you gave up your house—"

"That trailer wasn't much. Believe me I didn't mind giving it up. This is my home now," she said, glancing around the spacious kitchen.

"But it's not yours," Hannah protested.

"It doesn't take my name on a deed to make it feel like home. For that matter, I love my job. Dev Hart is my employer. But he never makes me feel like an employee, except for setting up a generous benefit package for me. Hannah, he's like the son I never had. And Ben—" She shook her head as her eyes grew suspiciously bright. "He's not a job. He's a joy."

"But, Mom—"

"No buts, Hannah. You're free to buy whatever you'd like. I know you've worked hard and you've certainly earned the right. But there's not a thing I need that money will buy. And as for moving to L.A., does the phrase when pigs fly mean anything to you?"

"I don't think I ever quite understood it, but I get your point," she said sadly.

It was clear that when Hannah returned to California, she would do it alone. How had everything she'd worked so long and so hard for gone so completely wrong? She'd always told herself brains and hard work would be enough. Hannah had gotten her dream job, and suddenly her dreams were falling apart.

Polly squeezed the hand she was still holding. "I belong here. I'm happy in Destiny."

In spite of the emotional blow, Hannah felt a smile tug at the corners of her mouth. "That happiness doesn't by any chance have something to do with a certain handsome, distinguished doctor, does it?"

Something happened that she had never in a million years expected to see. Polly Morgan blushed like a schoolgirl. Good heavens! Hannah suddenly got it. Money and material possessions didn't constitute a life. It was people who made us happy. Her mother might have had a rough time of it when Hannah was growing up, but she was making up for it now. And Hannah had tried to take her away from that.

Polly turned back to the sink and started to industriously scrub a perfectly clean pot. "I like Frank very much," was all she said.

"Are you going out?"

"He takes me to dinner and movies," she admitted.

"No. I mean *going out*. I believe the currently politically correct term is going steady."

With bright red cheeks, her mother made a most unladylike sound. "We're good friends."

"How good?" Hannah asked. "Do I need to have a talk with him? Do I need to ask him his intentions? Do I need to challenge him to stethoscopes at ten paces?"

"Only if you've changed your mind and decided to take him up on his offer of that partnership." When her mother turned and met her gaze, there was hope shining big and bright in her blue eyes.

"Mom, does that mean you want me to accept the position?" she asked softly.

"That's not my baby to rock," she said. "All I'll say is you look as sad as if you were sent for and couldn't go." She tipped her head to the side. "Or maybe you look like you lost your only friend because you were sent for and *could* go."

"Like I said, I've already accepted the job."

"You didn't put anything in writing?"

Hannah shook her head. "But I gave them my verbal acceptance of the job."

"So you tell them you changed your mind. It's not like you were the only candidate."

"I've spent my whole life trying to fit in, to find credibility."

"I could be wrong, sweetheart, but it seems to me you've accomplished that since you've been back in Destiny."

As far as Dev was concerned, Hannah had never felt less like she belonged. And she'd never wanted it more. "Mom, you taught me to be independent. That's what I'm being."

"You learned the right lesson. You're just going about it the wrong way. A woman needs to be prepared to take care of herself. That doesn't mean she has to go through life alone."

"Then why did you?"

"A lot of reasons. I was busy." She turned back to the sink and stared out the window. "There was you. And I didn't want to be hurt." Polly looked at her with sad eyes. "I'm afraid that by example I taught you another wrong lesson."

"What's that?"

"Don't take a chance. Protect yourself so no one can hurt you."

The way Hannah felt right now, she figured she'd completely bombed that course. She could only hope that distance and time would heal the damage to her heart.

"It's not such a bad lesson to learn, Mom."

Polly shook her head. "It is a bad lesson. I'm afraid I've cost you any chance for personal happiness. I think you *want* to accept Frank's offer and stay. But you're scared of your feelings for Dev."

Hannah plucked at the fibers in the dishrag. "Don't be silly, Mom."

"I don't think I am. And I've got a news flash for you. Not all men are tumbleweeds in the wind like your father."

"I know that."

"Do you? Is that why you're turning your back on a fine man? Dev Hart is stable, loyal, loving. He has roots that run too deep to pull. And he's got a face pretty enough to put on one of those Hollywood magazines. Are your standards a shade too high? What's not to like, Hannah?"

"Nothing."

"Look, honey, I've kept my mouth shut because sometimes that's what a mother has to do. And believe me you haven't made it easy. But I heard Ben say he saw his daddy kissing you. Twice." She pulled her hand out of the dishwater and held up two fingers to make a dripping V.

"It didn't mean anything," Hannah said defensively. "He wanted to show Ben that life isn't like a fairy tale and that I was still going to leave."

"Both times?" Polly asked skeptically.

"I'm not sure about the second time," Hannah admitted. "That came out of the blue."

"Did you like it?" Polly fixed a stern look on her. "I'll know if you lie to me."

"I wouldn't do that. I liked it more than anything." And even though she'd promised it wouldn't happen a third time, more than anything Hannah wanted to kiss him again.

"So what are you waiting for? An engraved invitation to stick around?"

"He's never asked me to stay." Hannah felt the sting of tears in her eyes.

Her mother stared at her as if she were sixteen years old and had just said she couldn't tie her shoes. "That's it? You're determined to hightail it back to California, thumbing your nose at a chance for happiness because he didn't ask you to stay?"

"He said the town could use my medical skills but he never once said *he* wanted me to stay." Hannah blinked and sniffled.

Her mother shook her head and sighed. "Honey, I guess you *were* behind the barn door when brains were being passed out."

"You make me sound like the class moron."

"When it comes to love and relationships, you are. There's just no way to sweeten that one, honey. You've been so busy getting an education that you haven't taken the time to learn about relationships."

"It was a distraction I couldn't afford."

"Well you can afford it now," her mother said dryly. "And here's something to think about. The woman he loved changed the rules after the 'I do's.' He lost the mother of his child to a career even after he put aside his pride and pleaded with her to stay.

He's not going to go there again. He'll throw the baby out with the bathwater first.''

"So you think he cares about me?''

"All I'm saying is that you should talk to him—really talk—before you turn your back. Promise me before you do that, you'll really think about what I said.''

"I'll go find him.''

But facing him would be more difficult than a microbiology final. In spite of her best efforts, she'd hurt his son. She'd opened up a deep wound for Dev. She would talk to him.

But the real question was—would he speak to her?

Chapter Twelve

Dev was standing by the corral fence, his arms folded on top as he stared at the star-filled sky. He'd tucked Ben into bed and tried to make his boy understand why Hannah had to go when he didn't understand it either. How could he let her leave?

He loved her.

Then he heard the sound of light footsteps behind him and somehow knew who it was. His gut clenched as he braced for impact.

"Dev, can I talk to you?"

Hannah. What was there left to say?

He knew now he'd been harboring a young man's ideal dream of hearth, home and the woman in it wearing an apron. Hannah had made him see that in today's world a woman's traditional role had changed to include jobs and men had to compromise to accommodate that.

Hannah had a job now—fifteen hundred miles away. He'd known that's what she wanted even before that first day she'd arrived so it shouldn't come as a shock. But the pain he felt at the thought knifed through him—in spite of everything he'd done to avoid it. He'd tried to keep from falling for her because she never planned to stay. Looking up at the bright night sky, he wondered if he was destined to keep wishing on the wrong star.

"Dev?"

He drew in a long breath and turned around. She stood in front of him, her hair silver in the moonlight. She was so beautiful it hurt. "What do you want to talk about?"

"How's Ben?"

"He'll be okay."

"I never meant to hurt him."

"I know."

"Did you know my mother and Doc are an item?" she blurted out.

The corners of his mouth curved up almost against his will. In spite of the pain crawling from his heart clear down to his soul, she could make him smile. "Yeah. I kind of had my suspicions. He spends a lot of time here at the ranch."

"You could have said something to me."

"Why?"

"Because I feel like an idiot. I've been making plans for her when she has plenty of plans of her own. You let me go on about giving her the good life knowing she had feelings for Doc."

"So what did she say? About you giving her the easy life, I mean?" he asked.

"That should be a no-brainer for you. She doesn't want it." Hannah moved beside him and leaned her back against the corral fence. "She made me see that

I'm not responsible for her happiness. She likes her life and she won't move to California. That should make you happy."

"Why do you say that?"

"You won't lose your housekeeper and child care for Ben."

"I want Polly to be happy—first and foremost. She's more to me than just an employee and you know it," he snapped.

"I'm sorry," she said. "It's just a lot to take in. And I'm concerned about her. Do you think they're in love?" she asked him.

"How the hell should I know? No way do I feel qualified to comment on Polly and Doc. It's *not* a no-brainer for a guy like me. I'm a rancher, not a relationship counselor. Besides, I messed up on love once." Actually twice, but there was no point in telling her that.

"I don't think you need to take all the responsibility for what happened in your marriage," Hannah said.

"Maybe not. But Corie was very young."

"And you were the wise old man?" she said with a smile.

"Something like that." It hurt too much to look at her. He glanced away and stared straight ahead into the blackness. "She brought out all my protective instincts. Something happened ten years ago. A bunch of us were at the lake and—"

"What?" Hannah asked.

"The details aren't important," he said. "But it was a lesson to us—"

"Us?"

"Me. Mitch. Jack Riley and Grady O'Connor. Girls—women are vulnerable. They need to be taken care of. So when I met Corie, she was so young, so pretty—" he shrugged. "She made me want to take care of her."

"I think that's very sweet."

"Yeah. I'm just a sweetheart of a guy."

"Don't be so hard on yourself."

"Why not? I was older. You said it yourself—I *should* have been the wise old man. But I mistook wanting to protect her for love. And I pushed too hard to get what I thought I wanted."

"And you got it?" she prompted.

"Yeah. I got it all right." He rubbed the back of his neck. "Unfortunately I steamrolled her and she didn't get a chance to tell me what *she* wanted. I had no idea she was even thinking about a career."

She touched his arm. "You can't take responsibility for the fact that she didn't speak up and say that her dream didn't match yours."

"Yeah. And what a joke. A woman who stays at home with the children and cooks and keeps house. It sounds old-fashioned."

"It's not a joke. In a perfect world it sounds ideal," she said.

"It's all I knew. And call me a male chauvinist pig, but it worked for me." He met her gaze. "You made me see that times have changed."

"Me? Really?"

He nodded. "I finally realized that Corie and me— our relationship—geography didn't tank us. Or her wanting a career. We didn't make it because she didn't love me enough." He stopped short of saying the critical words—to stay.

"So *now* what do you want?" she asked, a hopeful note in her voice.

To not let you go, he thought. To not hurt this bad at the prospect of a life without her. A do over. A chance to start from the beginning and not hurt her or make an ass of himself spouting that women are meant to be in the home, barefoot and pregnant.

"I want—"

He didn't want. He *needed* Hannah. But he'd made the mistake of being a dimwit once. No one could accuse him of not learning his lesson. He wouldn't beg her to stay for Ben—for him. If she did, it would have to be what she wanted.

"What do you want?" she prompted.

"I want Destiny to grow and prosper."

She blinked at him. "Sounds like a bad episode of *Star Trek*."

Dev wouldn't ask her to stay. But he figured it couldn't hurt to tip the scales in his favor. "You know what I mean. Mitch has a development company. He's working on improving the area. Houses, shopping, industry, entertainment. It's already a great environment, but things will only get better."

"Is that so?" Hannah knew when she'd been sidestepped. But he didn't tell her that he *didn't* want her. He'd just changed the subject.

"Yeah." He leaned back against the fence and stared down at her. "We've got wide open spaces, clean water and air. Kids can grow up with lots of land and animals. But it wouldn't hurt to have places to go and things to do either. We're on our way. Don't you think it would be exciting to be in on the beginning of that? More prosperity means more people who need health care.''

''Excuse me?''

''Didn't you take an oath?'' he asked.

''I did. But I don't think it started 'live long and prosper.'''

''All I'm trying to say is that there's more to life than what money can buy,'' he said.

Hannah had followed him outside to apologize for hurting his son. She'd also thought about what her mother had said, about taking the partnership Doc had offered her. But she loved Dev. He was wonderful— handsome, caring, easy to talk to, and with an above-average sense of humor. He'd helped her put the past into perspective. There was only one problem with that. Now there was nowhere left to hide. If Dev turned his back on her, she didn't think she would ever get over it. Letting her guard down could be on the top ten list of dumb things to do.

''What are you trying to tell me?'' she asked, hoping he would declare his undying love and the fact that he wouldn't survive if she left.

''I'm saying that Destiny is a great place and is on the brink of getting better. That's all.''

''Okay, then.'' She nodded. ''I'm glad you clarified that. But there's something I need to clarify. I came from nothing and made something of myself through a combination of planning and intelligence. Abandoning my career plan now wouldn't be terribly bright.''

''Are you saying Destiny would be a step down?''

''No. Let me say this in terms you can relate to. Altering my intended course at this late juncture would be like changing horses in midstream. I think you can see how that's not the smartest thing to do.''

''Yeah. Even I know enough to pour water out of a boot. I may not be in your league, but I can see a thing or two.''

''Such as?'' she asked, lifting her chin slightly.

''Such as you may have an IQ bigger than the state of Texas, but that doesn't change the fact that you're still scared.''

''What would I have to be scared of?'' But she knew.

''Being hurt.'' He took a big breath. ''I never met your father, but it occurs to me that you must be like him.''

''Why in the world would you say that?''

''You don't have the guts to stand and fight. You're running away—just like he did.''

''How dare you—''

''If the boot fits—or should I say stethoscope?''

Anger and pain twisted together inside her and she turned her back on Dev with every intention of walking away. Then it hit her. He was right. Maybe not about the part that she was just like her father. But she *was* running.

It was time to stop. Dev had helped her put her past into perspective. Now it was time to put it behind her. In that moment, she knew exactly what she had to do. The weight lifted from her heart. With crystal clarity, she realized that it was what would make her happy.

She turned back and calmly met his gaze. ''You're right. I am running. And I'm tired of being a loner geek. It's time to stop both. You were right about there being more to life than money. There's personal happiness and satisfaction—and fitting in with the community. Putting down roots and letting them dig in and grow too deep to pull. I've decided to accept Doc's offer and stay in Destiny.''

"Good.''

"Good? That's all you can say?''

"I could say this is so sudden?''

"It might look that way. But I have a feeling it's what I was after all along. I could have stayed in California and found work anywhere while I waited to hear about the job I thought I wanted. Somehow I knew I needed to come home. Working with Doc is the right thing for me.''

"Your mother must be happy.''

"She doesn't know yet.'' She glared at him. "I was sort of hoping *you'd* be happy I'm staying.''

Finally she put her hands on her hips. They'd reached an impasse. He wouldn't comment on her decision; she wouldn't tell him she cared. Each was expecting the other to blink first. To break down, break the ice, draw first blood. Well, she'd turned over a new leaf tonight. It was time to put up or shut up. Now or never. She would take a chance.

She moved close to him and rested her hand on his arm. "Obviously what we have here isn't a failure to communicate. It's fear of communication.''

"Is that so?'' One corner of his mouth lifted.

"Apparently neither of us wants to say it first. *I'm* going to be the mature one. That way, I can feel superior for the rest of our lives. I can hold it over your head—''

Suddenly, Dev pulled her into his arms. He held her as if he would never let her go, and looked into her eyes with such intensity it made her head spin. Everything she'd been about to say went right out of her mind. Her pulse raced and her heart pounded. Heat filled her and she couldn't seem to get close enough to him. Communication was an overrated skill. Actions spoke so much louder than words. She stood on tiptoe, waiting for him to touch her lips with his own.

But he took a deep breath and opened his mouth. "I love you, Hannah. Don't ever forget who said it first."

She blinked, then grinned. "I love you, Dev. And I don't care who said it first as long as we both know I intended to."

"Okay."

Happiness bubbled up inside her. Again she felt a sense of peace—that she and Dev were right together. But she needed to know for sure. She searched his gaze for any sign of doubt. "Are you certain? You saw firsthand that a doctor's life isn't easy. Sometimes patients have to come first."

"You're a good doctor, that's what I saw. Folks need you. Do what you need to. I don't care if you bake or whether or not you're there when I come home as long as you come home too—to me. I'll take whatever you have to give. I faced the emptiness of my life without you." Gently he tightened his hold on her. "Having you on any terms is heaven compared to not having you at all."

"Are you asking me to stay?"

"I swore I wouldn't—not even for Ben." He hugged her close for a moment, then drew back and looked into her eyes. "Hell yes, I'm asking you to stay. Don't leave me, Hannah. Heal my heart. Make me whole. Let me make you happy. Make me the happiest cowboy in Texas. Marry me. Please.''

"Oh, Dev.'' Her eyes blurred with moisture at his words. When a tear trickled down her cheek, he took her face between his big, calloused palms and brushed it away with his thumb.

"Don't keep me in suspense. My whole future depends on what that tear means. Is it a yes?''

She nodded. "I would like nothing better than to marry you. Third time's the charm.''

"What?''

"You've kissed me twice. We need number three,'' she said.

"It'd be my pleasure to oblige, ma'am.''

Cradling her face in his hands, he lowered his mouth to hers. The touch was gentle yet filled with so much passion and promise.

Hannah already felt like the luckiest woman in the world. She hadn't thought it was possible to have it all, but she did. A handsome cowboy who loved her, a satisfying career and a ready-made family. She knew their forever love and lifetime commitment was sealed with their third-time's-the-charm kiss.

He lifted his head and smiled at her. "I suppose that cancels out our agreement not to kiss again.''

"Okay,'' she agreed happily.

"Thank God.'' He let out a long, relieved breath, then kissed her forehead.

She rested her cheek against his chest and heard the steady beating of his heart. "You know, Ben was right all along. That very first kiss got my attention and started me thinking about staying. It changed my life, just like in the movies.''

"He'll be glad to hear that."

She looked at him. "We should go tell him and my mother."

"Soon. First there's something I need to say." He held her close, his lips a whisper away from hers. "I pledge to you my heart, my love, my life. I will make you the happiest woman in Destiny."

His lips touched hers and their promise of happy ever after was sealed with this kiss.

* * * * *

Look for Teresa Southwick's
next book, book three
of the DESTINY, TEXAS series,
coming in December
from Silhouette Romance.

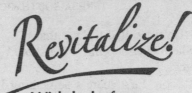

If you enjoyed what you just read,
then we've got an offer you can't resist!

Take 2 bestselling
love stories FREE!
Plus get a FREE surprise gift!

Clip this page and mail it to Silhouette Reader Service™

IN U.S.A.
3010 Walden Ave.
P.O. Box 1867
Buffalo, N.Y. 14240-1867

IN CANADA
P.O. Box 609
Fort Erie, Ontario
L2A 5X3

YES! Please send me 2 free Silhouette Romance® novels and my free surprise gift. After receiving them, if I don't wish to receive anymore, I can return the shipping statement marked cancel. If I don't cancel, I will receive 6 brand-new novels every month, before they're available in stores! In the U.S.A., bill me at the bargain price of $3.15 plus 25¢ shipping and handling per book and applicable sales tax, if any*. In Canada, bill me at the bargain price of $3.50 plus 25¢ shipping and handling per book and applicable taxes**. That's the complete price and a savings of at least 10% off the cover prices—what a great deal! I understand that accepting the 2 free books and gift places me under no obligation ever to buy any books. I can always return a shipment and cancel at any time. Even if I never buy another book from Silhouette, the 2 free books and gift are mine to keep forever.

215 SEN DFNQ
315 SEN DFNR

Name	(PLEASE PRINT)	
Address	Apt.#	
City	State/Prov.	Zip/Postal Code

* Terms and prices subject to change without notice. Sales tax applicable in N.Y.
** Canadian residents will be charged applicable provincial taxes and GST.
All orders subject to approval. Offer limited to one per household and not valid to current Silhouette Romance® subscribers.
® are registered trademarks of Harlequin Enterprises Limited.

SROM01
©1998 Harlequin Enterprises Limited

SILHOUETTE® MAKES YOU A STAR!

Feel like a star with Silhouette.

We will fly you and a guest to New York City for an exciting weekend stay at a glamorous 5-star hotel. Experience a refreshing day at one of New York's trendiest spas and have your photo taken by a professional. Plus, receive $1,000 U.S. spending money!

Flowers...long walks...dinner for two... how does Silhouette Books make romance come alive for you?

Send us a script, with 500 words or less, along with visuals (only drawings, magazine cutouts or photographs or combination thereof). Show us how Silhouette Makes Your Love Come Alive. Be creative and have fun. No purchase necessary. All entries must be clearly marked with your name, address and telephone number. All entries will become property of Silhouette and are not returnable. **Contest closes September 28, 2001.**

Please send your entry to: **Silhouette Makes You a Star!**

In U.S.A.
P.O. Box 9069
Buffalo, NY, 14269-9069

In Canada
P.O. Box 637
Fort Erie, ON, L2A 5X3

Look for contest details on the next page, by visiting www.eHarlequin.com or request a copy by sending a self-addressed envelope to the applicable address above. Contest open to Canadian and U.S. residents who are 18 or over. Void where prohibited.

Silhouette®
Where love comes alive™

Our lucky winner's photo will appear in a Silhouette ad. Join the fun!

SRMYAS1

HARLEQUIN "SILHOUETTE MAKES YOU A STAR!" CONTEST 1308
OFFICIAL RULES
NO PURCHASE NECESSARY TO ENTER

1. To enter, follow directions published in the offer to which you are responding. Contest begins June 1, 2001, and ends on September 28, 2001. Entries must be postmarked by September 28, 2001, and received by October 5, 2001. Enter by hand-printing (or typing) on an 8 ½" x 11" piece of paper your name, address (including zip code), contest number/name and attaching a script containing <u>500 words</u> or less, <u>along with drawings, photographs or magazine cutouts, or combinations thereof</u> (i.e., collage) <u>on no larger than 9" x 12"</u> piece of paper, describing how the <u>Silhouette books make romance come alive for you.</u> Mail via first-class mail to: Harlequin "Silhouette Makes You a Star!" Contest 1308, (in the U.S.) P.O. Box 9069, Buffalo, NY 14269-9069, (in Canada) P.O. Box 637, Fort Erie, Ontario, Canada L2A 5X3. Limit one entry per person, household or organization.

2. Contests will be judged by a panel of members of the Harlequin editorial, marketing and public relations staff. Fifty percent of criteria will be judged against script and fifty percent will be judged against drawing, photographs and/or magazine cutouts. Judging criteria will be based on the following:

   - Sincerity—25%
   - Originality and Creativity—50%
   - Emotionally Compelling—25%

   In the event of a tie, duplicate prizes will be awarded. Decisions of the judges are final.

3. All entries become the property of Torstar Corp. and may be used for future promotional purposes. Entries will not be returned. No responsibility is assumed for lost, late, illegible, incomplete, inaccurate, nondelivered or misdirected mail.

4. Contest open only to residents of the U.S. (except Puerto Rico) and Canada who are 18 years of age or older, and is void wherever prohibited by law; all applicable laws and regulations apply. Any litigation within the Province of Quebec respecting the conduct or organization of a publicity contest may be submitted to the Régie des alcools, des courses et des jeux for a ruling. Any litigation respecting the awarding of a prize may be submitted to the Régie des alcools, des courses et des jeux only for the purpose of helping the parties reach a settlement. Employees and immediate family members of Torstar Corp. and D. L. Blair, Inc., their affiliates, subsidiaries and all other agencies, entities and persons connected with the use, marketing or conduct of this contest are not eligible to enter. Taxes on prizes are the sole responsibility of the winner. Acceptance of any prize offered constitutes permission to use winner's name, photograph or other likeness for the purposes of advertising, trade and promotion on behalf of Torstar Corp., its affiliates and subsidiaries without further compensation to the winner, unless prohibited by law.

5. Winner will be determined no later than November 30, 2001, and will be notified by mail. Winner will be required to sign and return an Affidavit of Eligibility/Release of Liability/Publicity Release form within 15 days after winner notification. Noncompliance within that time period may result in disqualification and an alternative winner may be selected. All travelers must execute a Release of Liability prior to ticketing and must possess required travel documents (e.g., passport, photo ID) where applicable. Trip must be booked by December 31, 2001, and completed within one year of notification. No substitution of prize permitted by winner. Torstar Corp. and D. L. Blair, Inc., their parents, affiliates and subsidiaries are not responsible for errors in printing of contest, entries and/or game pieces. In the event of printing or other errors that may result in unintended prize values or duplication of prizes, all affected game pieces or entries shall be null and void. **Purchase or acceptance of a product offer does not improve your chances of winning.**

6. Prizes: (1) Grand Prize—A 2-night/3-day trip for two (2) to New York City, including round-trip coach air transportation nearest winner's home and hotel accommodations (double occupancy) at The Plaza Hotel, a glamorous afternoon makeover at <u>a trendy New York spa</u>, $1,000 in U.S. spending money and an opportunity to <u>have a professional photo taken and appear in a Silhouette advertisement</u> (approximate retail value: $7,000). (10) Ten Runner-Up Prizes of gift packages (retail value $50 ea.). Prizes consist of only those items listed as part of the prize. Limit one prize per person. Prize is valued in U.S. currency.

7. For the name of the winner (available after December 31, 2001) send a self-addressed, stamped envelope to: Harlequin "Silhouette Makes You a Star!" Contest 1197 Winners, P.O. Box 4200 Blair, NE 68009-4200 or you may access the www.eHarlequin.com Web site through February 28, 2002.

Contest sponsored by Torstar Corp., P.O Box 9042, Buffalo, NY 14269-9042.

SRMYAS2

SILHOUETTE Romance

COMING NEXT MONTH

#1546 THE MISSING MAITLAND—Stella Bagwell
Maitland Maternity: The Prodigal Children
A mysterious man rescued TV reporter Blossom Woodward—and then kidnapped her! Blossom's nose for news knew there was more to Larkin the handyman than what he claimed…was he the missing Maitland they'd been searching for? Only *close* questioning could uncover the truth…!

#1547 WHEN THE LIGHTS WENT OUT…—Judy Christenberry
Having the Boss's Baby
Scared of small spaces, Sharon Davies turned to a stranger when she was stranded in an elevator, and got to know him *intimately*. Months later, she nearly fainted when she met her boss's biggest client. How could she tell Jack their time in the dark had created a little bundle of joy?

#1548 WORKING OVERTIME—Raye Morgan
Temporarily sharing a house with a woman and her toddlers awoke painful memories in Michael Greco, and sharing an office created more tension! The brooding tycoon tried to avoid Chareen Wolf and her sons, but eluding the boys was one thing—resisting their alluring mother was more difficult….

#1549 A GIRL, A GUY AND A LULLABY—Debrah Morris
A friend was all aspiring singer Ryanne Rieger was looking for when she returned to her hometown broke, disillusioned and pregnant. She found one in rancher Tom Hunnicutt. But Tom wouldn't be content with *just* friends—and could Ryanne ever let herself give more…?

#1550 TEN WAYS TO WIN HER MAN—Beverly Bird
Sparks flew the moment Danielle Harrington and Maxwell Padgett met. Strong willed and used to getting her own way, Danielle tried everything she could to make successful and sophisticated Max fall for her, except the one thing guaranteed to win his heart: being herself!

#1551 BORN TO BE A DAD—Martha Shields
Good Samaritan Rick McNeal became a temporary dad because of an accident. When Kate Burnett and little Joey needed a home, the lonely widower opened his door—but would he ever open his heart?

RSCNM0901